Audra - The Prequel

Delaney Diamond

Garden Avenue Press

Audra – The Prequel by Delaney Diamond

Copyright © January 2025, Delaney Diamond

Garden Avenue Press

Atlanta, Georgia

978-1-946302-86-1 (Ebook edition)

978-1946302-69-4 (Paperback edition)

www.delaneydiamond.com

Chapter One

"How do I look?"

Claudia, Audra's friend and co-worker, checked her appearance in the mirrored door of the elevator, puckering her lips and then turning around to examine the fit of the dress on her backside.

"You look fantastic," Audra said.

Claudia's outfit was perfect for the springtime weather during the first week of April. She wore a hot pink bandeau dress that matched her hot pink lipstick, and her blonde hair fell midway down her back in glossy waves.

Audra, on the other hand, looked plain in purple shorts and a white sleeveless top, which she didn't regret wearing. She hadn't wanted to come to this party in the first place.

She shouldn't have let Claudia talk her into coming, but what else did she have to do on a Saturday afternoon? And Claudia didn't want to come alone. She'd had a big fight with her long distance boyfriend, and when a friend of a friend told her about the get-together, she saw it as an opportunity to meet and nab a man in town.

1

Of course, Claudia didn't listen to Audra when she warned that athletes—celebrity males in general—were not exactly the kind of men she should consider for a serious relationship. Audra knew this from firsthand experience.

"I don't know why I'm so nervous." Claudia laughed and sent a quick glance her way.

"Because you're hoping to pick up a man while we're here, knowing full well you and Kent are going to make up and this will all have been a waste of time."

Claudia pouted her pink lips. "You're wrong. We're not making up this time. I'm done with him."

The doors opened on the top floor where the party was taking place, at some baseball player's condo. Members of the team were celebrating the end of spring training and the pending start of the season.

Since Audra didn't pay attention to sports, she had already forgotten the nickname Claudia said the fans called the host. She vaguely remembered his name meant fast. Was it Lightning....? Mr. Speed? She wasn't sure.

They walked down the hallway to a door marked with the number eleven-fifty in gold. Music thumped from the inside, and Claudia turned to Audra with excitement in her eyes. She shimmied her shoulders before she rang the doorbell, and almost immediately, a tall white guy with dark hair and a five o'clock shadow swung open the door from the inside.

Is this him—The Rapid One? Audra wondered, trying another name that didn't sound right, either.

"Well hello, ladies," he crooned, his eyes practically devouring Claudia. He stepped aside. "Come on in and welcome to the party."

"Thank you," Claudia smiled up at him as she sidled past.

Audra followed, hiding her amusement. Claudia was a master at flirting.

There were a few dozen people in attendance, mostly women dressed in revealing outfits. Her discerning eyes flicked over the decor. She saw white—walls, furniture, and most of the furnishings, which she figured wouldn't withstand the party atmosphere. What wasn't white was black. Outside the large windows was a balcony where some of the partygoers had congregated, looking out over the city and the highway nearby.

"I'm Jacob, by the way, and you are..." Jacob extended a hand to Claudia.

"Claudia, and this is my friend, Audra."

"Nice to meet you both. What can I get you ladies to drink?" He held on to Claudia's hand, and her friend didn't pull away.

"I'd like something fruity," she said.

"I will make you something fruity," Jacob promised. "Do you have a specific drink in mind?"

"Surprise me." Claudia twirled a lock of hair around her finger.

"Will do. And what can I get for you, Audra?"

"Coke is fine," she replied.

"A non-drinker. Smart woman. I'll be right back." Jacob winked and strutted away.

"You're being real subtle," Audra teased.

"I told you I came here to get a man, and I meant it," Claudia said out the corner of her mouth. "Let's see what other fine specimens are available for me to sink my claws into."

They strolled through the large room. The men in attendance were definitely good-looking and in excellent shape. Audra suspected most, if not all of them were athletes. *Maybe I should pay more attention to baseball*, she mused.

She helped herself to a nacho at one of the food tables. As she was crunching the snack between her teeth, her gaze wandered toward the balcony doors.

She froze.

There was a man standing there, dressed casually in chinos and a snug-fitting burnt ochre shirt that showed off his defined chest and exposed tattooed arms. Clearly one of the athletes.

A diamond stud sparkled in his left ear, a striking contrast to his milk chocolate skin. A mustache connected to a beard formed a circle around his mouth—neat and low the way she liked. He looked tall, but everyone looked tall because she was short. His casual sexiness caught her off guard and made her stare. He looked like he spent a lot of time on his appearance and probably smelled good too.

He was looking at her—blatantly, openly. The way he looked at her made her knees soften and almost give way. Her whole body tingled under his watchful gaze.

Jacob approached with their drinks and blocked her view of the man by the door. He handed Claudia a red, slushy drink that looked like a daiquiri. Audra took her Coke.

While Claudia and Jacob flirted, her eyes searched for the hot guy but didn't see him. Feeling like a third wheel, she interrupted her friend's conversation. "Excuse me, I need to make a quick phone call."

Claudia opened her mouth to say something, but Audra slipped away. For show, she pulled out her phone on the way to the kitchen. Other than the stainless steel appliances, the entire kitchen was white too.

"This guy needs a decorator," she muttered to herself.

There was extra food and snacks on the island, so she opened a bag of chips and munched on a few as she scrolled through her Twitter feed.

"Hiding?" The voice came from behind her, and she spun around, drawing a startled breath when she saw the hot guy standing several feet away. Damn, he was fine.

One hand held a tumbler of dark liquor. He put up the

other hand in a disarming way. "Sorry, I didn't mean to startle you."

"Don't worry about it. I was mesmerized by a Twitter war between a Democratic representative and a Republican senator."

His eyebrows shot higher. "Deep stuff to be looking into at a party."

"I needed a break from out there."

"You're not having a good time?"

Audra shrugged instead of answering honestly.

"Oh no." He laughed. Slow and sexy, which made her entire body vibrate with awareness.

"Honestly, I didn't want to come. I'm keeping my friend company."

"Oh, gotcha," he said, slowly nodding.

His probing eyes examined her from head to foot, and Audra felt her cheeks burn under his scrutiny.

"I'm Damon, by the way. Damon Foster."

Oddly, the way he pronounced his name and then waited gave her the impression that he expected her to say something afterward.

"Audra Connor. I guess you play baseball, like the owner of this place?"

He tilted his head and looked at her with an odd expression she didn't understand.

"Is there something wrong?" Audra asked.

He smirked. "Nah, it's... never mind. Yes, I play a little bit. It's nice to meet you, Audra."

"Nice to meet you." She shifted from one foot to the other, unsure what to say next. "Well, I guess I better head back out there. Excuse me."

As she moved toward him, he shifted out of the way and spilled some of his drink on the counter near the door. He swore softly.

"Careful now. With all this white on white, Shazam is already probably going to have to do a lot of cleaning when this party's over. Don't give him any more work to do."

He shot a confused look her way. "Did you say Shazam?"

"Yes, the guy who owns this place. His name is Shazam—or something, right?"

Damon ripped a sheet from the paper towel holder and sopped up the spilled drink. "Pretty sure his name's not Shazam."

"What is it then?"

"The Flash," he answered. "Some people say Flash for short."

She snapped her fingers. "I knew it was something like that. Fast, Mr. Rapido, something."

"Mr. Rapido? Wow." He continued to watch her with amusement. "You're not much of a baseball fan, huh?"

"I've never seen a game," she admitted.

"Interesting." His eyes narrowed slightly, as if he was trying to figure her out. "Your comment a second ago, about the color scheme. Was that a critique?"

"Far be it from me to criticize anyone's choices, but..." She looked around the kitchen and wrinkled her nose. "All the white everywhere and only black to break it up, makes the place seem kind of colorless and cold. But please don't tell Shazam—I mean, The Flash what I said. It's my opinion, and I'm sure he had his reasons for decorating the way he did."

"I'm sure he did. Don't worry, your secret's safe with me." With a twist of his fingers, he pretended to lock his mouth.

"Thank you." Audra cleared her throat. "Okay, I'm going to find my friend now."

"Sure. Nice meeting you, Audra."

"Nice to meet you too, Damon."

She walked out, knowing his eyes stayed on her the entire time. Being around Damon made her feel tense and awkward, as if she'd never spoken to a man before. Only once she was moving toward the middle of the room did she relax.

"There you are!" Claudia slipped an arm around her and drew her into a conversation with another woman.

Audra halfway listened to them, her mind elsewhere.

During the brief conversation with Damon, she had experienced more than awkwardness and tension. She experienced an emotion she hadn't felt in a long time.

Excitement.

There was something magnetic about him. Even now, a flutter of awareness hovered low in her stomach.

And like she had suspected, he smelled amazing.

Chapter Two

D amon watched Audra nursing her soda while chatting with her friend across the room. He had to admit to being smitten from the moment he saw her talking to Jacob and her friend.

What was it about her? She was attractive, but he had his pick of attractive women.

She was petite with broad hips, full luscious breasts, and an ample behind prominently displayed in purple shorts. Coupled with her white top, the ensemble showed off the deep brown of her skin—a color akin to the deepest, darkest brown sugar. Her radiant smile, as she laughed at something her friend said, enveloped not only her pretty lips, but took over her entire face.

What fascinated him most of all was that Audra didn't seem to be trying much. At least not as hard as some of the other women there. She didn't seem to be trying at all, and the fact that she didn't know who the hell he was intrigued him.

She glanced his way, her long thick hair swinging over one shoulder. Holding his breath, he was struck again by something electrifying. He smiled as his heart jerked out of control. She smiled back, letting her gaze drift away and back to her friend.

"Heyyyy, Flash." A sexy woman with copper-toned skin sidled up to him.

"Hey..." He hesitated to say her name because he realized he wasn't sure what her name was. Keisha? Tanisha?

"Lanisha," she said, arching an eyebrow.

"I knew that." A smile slid across his lips.

"Uh-huh." She didn't seem upset, which was good and bad. He didn't want her to be offended, but at the same time, women let him off the hook too much.

"You having a good time?" he asked.

"I'd have a better time if I could have a moment alone with you, to talk," she replied.

That's right, he had promised her alone time and flirted with her and several other women in attendance—before Audra showed up and jacked his attention like a mugger with a gun.

"Maybe later? I need to circulate a bit and make sure everyone's okay."

"I understand, but don't forget me." She trailed a hand down his tattooed arm.

"I won't." He watched her sashay away, her pert bottom looking extra nice in denim capris. Life was good.

When he swung his head in the direction of Audra, he didn't see her. His eyebrows snapped together. Where was she? She didn't leave, did she?

He turned in a complete circle, and when he still didn't see her, he walked over to Jacob. "Hey, have you seen Audra? She's a sexy chocolate sister. Kinda short. She was with a blonde in a hot pink dress."

"I wouldn't mind having some sexy chocolate."

"Did you see her or not?" Damon asked, not in the mood for his jokes.

Jacob smirked. "Why?" He took a sip of beer.

"I want to talk to her, that's all. I hope she hasn't left." He swiveled his head left to right, scanning the room.

As the sun was going down, more people had arrived, and his condo was packed, resembling a club-like atmosphere with the loud music. He didn't know most of these people, which under normal circumstances was fine, but Audra was short, and the crowded space made it difficult to find her.

"Are you in *love*?" Jacob teased.

"Goddamn, I want to talk to her, not marry her," Damon said irritably.

"You better not. All your other women will have a meltdown if you become monogamous."

"I don't have other women," Damon grumbled.

"Tell them that, not me." His friend chuckled. "To answer your question, I've seen Audra. She and her friend—Claudia—went out to the balcony. You better move fast if you want to get those digits. I saw Eddie heading out there, and you know he moves fast."

An unreasonable amount of animosity toward his friend waved through Damon. Eddie was probably the biggest player on the team, and he didn't discriminate when it came to race. If he saw a woman he was attracted to, he made a move on her. Damon couldn't allow his friend to swoop in on the one woman he was genuinely interested in.

With grim determination, he made his way toward the balcony, stopping a couple of times for a quick chat with guests. A number of people were outside, standing around or seated on the patio furniture—drinking, eating, and talking. He spotted Audra right away with her friend, and then there was Eddie, all up in their faces.

As he approached, Audra turned her eyes to him, which

prompted Eddie to look over his shoulder to see what had caught her attention.

Slapping his friend on the shoulder, Damon said, "What's up, Eddie? Everybody okay out here?" With the music locked behind the glass, conversation was easier.

"Yeah, I'm good, man." Eddie was actually Eduardo, a mixed-race Cuban with dark hair and swarthy skin. The ladies loved him and his damn accent.

"Ladies?" Damon kept his eyes on Audra.

"I'm okay," she said.

"Me too, although I could eat more of those shrimp things," her friend said with a laugh.

"There's plenty more of those in the kitchen. Eddie, could you show her where the food is? I'll keep Audra company." Hand still resting on Eddie's shoulder, he squeezed, sending a signal to his friend.

"Uh, yeah, *no problema*. I can do that. Claudia, *venga conmigo*." Eddie extended his arm.

Claudia shot a quick look at Audra, making sure she was okay being left alone with him.

"I'll be fine. I'll wait here," she said.

"Be right back." Claudia took Eddie's arm and let him escort her inside.

Damon took a moment to take in Audra—the luscious curves, the full sexy lips, the smooth dark skin, and her long hair. "You're still here."

"I decided to hang around a little longer. The food's good."

"That's the only reason?"

"And Claudia's my ride, so..." She shrugged.

Damn, Audra was going to be a tough nut to crack, but he was up for the challenge. Time to pour on the charm.

Damon leaned closer and lowered his voice. "Listen, I wasn't completely honest with you earlier."

"Oh?" One of her eyebrows climbed higher.

"I'm the owner of this condo and the host of the party. I'm The Flash. They call me that because I'm fast on the field."

She let out a cute laugh. "No, you're not. If you were The Flash, you would have told me."

"I'm telling you now."

The smile evaporated on her face, and the circumference of her eyes expanded. "Tell me you're joking. Please."

"I'm not. I'm Damon 'The Flash' Foster."

Her mouth slowly opened in shock, and all he could think about was tugging her lower lip between his teeth. Audra covered her face with one hand and muttered something that sounded like "Ohmigod."

Finally, she looked at him with embarrassment etched into her features. "I'm so sorry for getting your name wrong in the kitchen and the smart remark I made about your decorating. Actually, now that I think about it, I really like the minimalist approach."

Damon bit back a laugh. "Now you're lying."

She made an unconsciously sexy move, looking up at him with her big brown eyes and sinking her teeth into the corner of her mouth. His eyes dipped for a second to her lips. He was jealous of her teeth.

"Don't worry, I've been called worse things than Shazam. I thought it was pretty funny. But, if you want to make up for your bad behavior... how about you let me take you out to dinner." He locked eyes with her.

She seemed taken aback and let out a soft laugh, averting her gaze to the parking lot below.

"What did I say that was funny?" Damon asked.

"I'm flattered, but I'm not interested."

She was actually turning him down. Huh. That was new. Now *he* was the one taken aback.

"Why not? You think I'm ugly or something?"

"No!"

He almost busted out laughing at her mortified expression.

"Actually," she continued in a careful voice, "you're very handsome, but... let's be honest, okay? You could have your pick of any woman here. Matter of fact, I've seen you in action, flirting and whatnot. You have plenty of choices at this party."

"I'm not going to deny I have options, but I'm not interested in the other women here. I'm interested in you, Audra Connor." He continued to make eye contact so there would be no question about his sincerity.

"I can't."

"Why not?" Damon asked. Heat flushed his neck because he was starting to sound desperate.

"Because..." She paused, then seemed to change her mind about what she planned to say. "I'm not interested in getting involved with anyone right now. To be honest, you remind me too much of my ex."

"He's handsome, funny, and filthy rich?"

She laughed again, and it was the prettiest sound. "No. He's untrustworthy and not into commitment." The resigned sadness in her voice cut through him.

Some other man had messed things up for him. Bastard.

"I'm nothing like that," Damon insisted.

Okay, maybe that wasn't exactly true. Commitment was a foreign word to him, but he could be trustworthy. He tended to lay his cards on the table. Most women understood he wasn't a one-woman man. Why would he be? He was only twenty-seven years old, in the prime of his life and the peak of his career. Settling down was the furthest thing from his mind.

"I'm sure you're a great guy, Mr. Flash."

"Mr. Flash?"

"Damon." A teasing smile lifted the corners of her mouth.

She was messing with him. "But I don't date famous men, or men chasing fame. They come with too many negatives. It's nothing personal."

"So that's it? There's nothing I can do or say to change your mind?"

"I'm afraid not."

Claudia and Eddie returned, both of them carrying small plates of the shrimp tartlets the caterer had made for the party. They were always a hit.

"These are so good," Claudia popped one in her mouth.

"I better get some before they're all gone. Come show me where they are." Audra dragged a stumbling Claudia behind her and back inside.

Eddie sauntered closer. "Struck out, *hermano*?"

Damon stared after them until they disappeared among the rest of the guests. "I never strike out. I ain't even gone up to bat yet."

Chapter Three

Claudia pulled her car to the front of the house.

"All right, girl, I'll see you on Monday." Audra pushed open the passenger side door.

"Did you have a good time?" Claudia asked before Audra could get out.

"I had a wonderful time. The *best*," Audra said with exaggerated enthusiasm.

"Audra." Claudia stuck out her lower lip.

She laughed and pulled her friend into a one-armed hug. "I'm kidding! I had a great time. It was good to get out of the house for a bit."

Claudia's face brightened. "That's better. I had a good time, *and* I have two phone numbers in my purse."

"Uh-oh, watch out, Kent!"

Claudia tossed her blonde hair. "His loss. See you on Monday."

"Bye, girl." Audra climbed out, and Claudia honked on her way down the long driveway.

Audra climbed the stairs and let herself into the house. The house her stepfather had built for their large family was a big change from their life from before, when Audra's single-parent mother had been struggling to raise three children after the death of her husband. Eventually, Audra wanted to move out and get her own place and was currently saving money for that day.

She closed the door and took the stairs up to her room. It was only a little after nine, so she was surprised by the quiet of the house.

Her bedroom was filled with candles and decorated in soft neutrals like ivory and camel. She was kicking off her shoes when the door behind her opened, and her free-spirited sister, Monica, walked in. Monica, tall and thin as a supermodel, had her hair pulled back in a ponytail and tucked under into a sleek bun.

Audra gasped when she saw her. "What the heck are you doing here?" she asked, pulling her sister into a hug.

Monica laughed and squeezed her back. "Can't I come home to see my family?" She grinned and plopped onto Audra's bed. She was in her last year of college at the University of Georgia in Athens.

"I didn't expect you, that's all." Audra walked into her closet. "What's been up?"

"Nothing much. Classes kicking my butt, but I'll handle it. Where were you tonight?"

"One second." Audra changed into her navy pajama shorts set. Returning to the bedroom, she pulled her thick hair into a ponytail and sat cross-legged on the bed to face her sister. "I was at a party."

Monica arched an eyebrow. "A party? Since when do you party—although..." She checked her watch. "It's still pretty early."

"Well, it wasn't a party-party. More like a get-together. I

went with Claudia, and people were still hanging out when we left. Honestly, I didn't want to go, but I'm glad I went. It was good to go out."

"Why didn't you want to go?" Monica asked.

"Because I knew there'd be a bunch of celebrities there. Not my scene."

"Papa Ben and Ignacio are celebrities," Monica pointed out, referring to their stepfather and stepbrother.

Benicio Santana had worked for years in the entertainment industry in Mexico, first as an actor and then as a director and producer. Ignacio was the only one of his sons to follow in his footsteps.

"That's different, and you know what I mean. Anyway, I had a good time. I should definitely go out more."

"Good for you."

Audra plucked at the sheet, toying with the idea of telling Monica about Damon. "I also kinda sorta met a guy."

"Kinda? Do tell." Monica leaned closer.

Audra lifted her hands. "Wait, nothing happened. We didn't exchange numbers or anything, but he was definitely... interesting."

"Why didn't you exchange numbers?"

"I didn't want to give him my number." Audra shrugged.

"The fact that you're mentioning him means you were feeling him, so what happened?"

"I don't know, Monica. I didn't go there to meet a man, and besides, I have Kerilyn," Audra said, referring to her daughter. "This guy I met, Damon, reminds me too much of—Kerry." She wrinkled her nose, hating to say her ex's name.

"Oh."

"Yeah."

She hadn't dated anyone seriously since she broke up with her daughter's father, and looking back, they had been in a one-sided relationship. She had been all in, while he had one foot out the entire time.

They had met when she was a senior in high school, and he'd dropped out of college to pursue his dream of making a living as a drummer in his Afropunk band. His wildness had matched hers. They were both young and a bit rebellious, but that changed when she became pregnant. She became more serious and wanted to be a good mother. Her daughter grounded her. Kerry, not so much.

He became scarce, barely a father or a boyfriend. While she dreamed of them living together as a family, he made it clear that touring and putting all his energy into the band was his priority.

They were off and on for a couple of years for Kerilyn's sake, but Audra became tired of his excuses and lack of interest in both of them. The photos he shared online didn't help. He was always hugged up with some woman, or a 'fan' was always draped over him like a human blanket while he grinned from ear to ear.

They never actually broke up, just drifted apart when she finally stopped trying to make something happen that was never going to happen. Her battered heart couldn't take any more pummeling.

"Damon, huh?" Monica said.

Audra nodded. "He plays for the Atlanta Braves. They call him The Flash."

Monica's eyes widened. "Holy smokes, I know who he is! He's hot, Audra. Are you sure—"

"Absolutely *not*. If I get involved with him, I'm pretty sure my life will be filled with drama. I know his type."

"Maybe, maybe not."

"Well, it's too late now. I told him I wasn't interested, and he moved on. He's probably laid up with one of the *many* women who were ogling him tonight." Unexpected envy filled her.

"They might have been ogling him, but it sounds like he was ogling you."

Audra blushed. "There will be other opportunities for me to meet a good man."

"True, and you're right. He's famous—not only for baseball."

"What do you mean?"

"You know how it is. He's young, wealthy, well known—and he takes full advantage of all the women that come his way. He's known as a bit of a player. I'm not sure I've seen him in a serious relationship." She frowned as she thought.

"You know all this and still thought it would be a good idea for me to get involved with this man?" Audra demanded.

"You don't have to marry him. He'd be nice for a quick fling," Monica replied with a coy expression.

"I'm not you. My feelings get caught up easily."

"True," Monica said.

Audra thumped her arm, and Monica cried out, rubbing the spot.

The door popped open and in waltzed Audra's six-year-old daughter in Minnie Mouse pajamas. Kerilyn was golden-skinned like her father and wore her hair in long plaits.

"Mommy!" She ran over, and Audra resettled on the bed, pulling her between her thighs to give her a hug and kiss.

"You missed me?"

"Yes!"

Audra plied kisses all over her face. "I missed you too, baby."

"Did you have fun?" Kerilyn asked, gazing up at her.

"I sure did. I ate too much food and met new people. You didn't give Grandma and *Abuelo* too much trouble, did you?"

"No. I was good." Kerilyn climbed up on the bed to sit between Audra and Monica.

"I think she's lying," Monica said.

"I'm not," Kerilyn insisted, laughing because she knew Monica was teasing.

"I don't believe you," Monica said.

She proceeded to tickle her niece. Kerilyn squirmed and wriggled, letting out gasping laughter until she scrambled to hide behind her mother.

Finally, Monica rose from the bed. "I'll leave you two alone. I need to get dressed."

"For what? Where are you headed at this hour?" Audra asked.

"It's not even ten o'clock yet. I'm going out, and that's all you need to know," Monica said with a smirk.

"Okay, Miss Thang."

Laughing, her sister left the bedroom.

Kerilyn flung her arms around Audra's neck from behind. "Can I sleep in your room tonight?"

Audra kissed her daughter's wrist. "Yes, you can. If you promise not to kick me in your sleep."

"I promise!" Kerilyn said immediately.

"Okay, you can sleep with me," Audra said, though she knew her daughter wouldn't live up to the promise.

Later, as Kerilyn slept soundly beside her in the bed, Audra remained wide awake. She couldn't stop thinking about Damon. Every time she saw him at the party, her eyes lingered. She liked to watch him walk. Considering he was called "The Flash," he didn't move quickly. His gait was smooth and graceful with a sprinkle of swagger.

"What the hell," she muttered.

Succumbing to temptation, she rolled over and plucked her phone from the bedside table. She searched for information on

Damon, clicking on article after article about him. She read about his prowess as a baseball player and his prowess as a ladies' man. The images of him online were as intriguing as the articles. Whether wearing a suit or casually dressed in jeans, he was eye-catching. Sexy, with a self-assured white-toothed smile and a diamond stud in his ear.

As she perused the photos, the lower part of her stomach became warm. She was definitely attracted to him. There were lots of photos of him, many of them with women—holding their hand as he led the way, smiling beside them at a red carpet event, hazy pictures of him at dinner with another one.

She sighed. Monica wasn't kidding. He was definitely a ladies' man.

She replaced the phone on the table. If the gossip blogs, tabloids, and magazines were correct, she'd dodged a bullet by avoiding him.

He was probably worse than her ex because he was richer, more handsome, and better known.

Chapter Four

"I am stuffed," Claudia moaned, rubbing her flat belly.

"Same. I shouldn't have eaten all that food, but it was so good," Audra said.

They had just returned from lunch at a nearby Italian restaurant. Bad idea. The rich sauces and heavy pasta made her want to curl up in a ball and take a nap instead of going back to work.

Both women were administrative assistants at Santana International, Audra's stepfather's company. Audra worked for one of the teams that provided marketing services for several of her stepfather's businesses and hoped to advance to join the team one day.

Claudia worked on the opposite side of the floor for a different team. She groaned as they strolled past the cubicles—some empty, others occupied with employees who had already returned from lunch.

"I should have never listened to you. You're such a bad influence," she muttered.

"Me? *You* insisted on going to lunch there. Next time you

make a bad suggestion, I'm going to remind you of this day—"
Audra pulled up short.

A huge bouquet of beautiful spring flowers sat on her desk.

"Wow," Claudia said. She shot Audra a look.

Audra frowned. Who in the world would send her flowers?
She approached the arrangement as if it was a hissing snake.
An older female employee walked up, her eyes alight with
curiosity. "What's the occasion?"

"There's no occasion," Audra replied, staring at the flowers.
It wasn't her birthday, and there was nothing special about the
date.

"Client, maybe?" the woman suggested.

"I doubt it. I guess there's only one way to find out." Audra
read the card.

I hope these flowers bring a smile to your face. - Flash

Her heart skipped through her chest at a faster rate.

"That smile says it all. Who is he?" Claudia tried to peer at
the card, but Audra hugged it to her chest.

"I was smiling?" she asked.

"Yes," the other employee said.

"Are you going to tell us who the flowers are from or not?"
Claudia demanded.

Audra looked at the older woman, and she looked at Audra.
There was a moment of awkward staring before the woman
shrugged and walked away.

Audra lowered her voice. "They're from the baseball player
at the party we went to over the weekend." She handed the
card to Claudia. "We didn't exchange numbers. How did he
find me?"

"Um... I might have had something to do with that."
Claudia returned the card.

"Excuse me?" Audra said.

"Don't get mad. Jacob and I talked on Sunday, and he asked

me questions about you that Damon wanted to know. Finally, I gave in. I told him you were single, but I couldn't give him your number. I did explain that we work at the same place." She grimaced, as if bracing for impact.

"Claudia..."

"I know, I know, but this is nice, isn't it? Not only did he try to get your attention at the party, he used one of his friends to get more information. Now the flowers. Audra, you must have made quite an impression."

"It's very flattering, but..."

"Give him a chance. Kent doesn't do anything like this. If he did, I would be all over him."

"Yeah, well, I'd love to find a good man to date, but I'm not sure this man is the right choice." Audra tucked her purse in her drawer.

"What could it possibly hurt?" Claudia asked.

If only she knew, getting involved could hurt quite a bit. Kerilyn's father had taught her a valuable lesson. Plus, Damon wasn't exactly her type. Too GQ. Too handsome. Too put together.

Her ex had dreadlocks and an untamed beard, and while he was taller than Damon, Damon was muscular where he was lanky. She suspected Kerilyn would end up tall like her father instead of staying short like Audra.

"He has plenty of women to keep him busy. He doesn't need me in the mix," Audra said.

"You could be the woman who makes him change his ways. You should go out with him."

"Thank you for the advice, but I know how to handle this," Audra said.

"Women like you make me sick!" Claudia hissed. "You have men falling all over you, and you're so blasé about it.

Teach me your ways." She pressed her hands together in fake prayer.

Audra brushed her away with a laugh and a wave of her hand. "I do not have men falling all over me. Stop being silly. You're the one who has men eating out of your hand."

"If I did, my man would behave and treat me better." Claudia spoke lightly, but Audra saw the shadow of disappointment nestled in her eyes.

She squeezed her friend's arm. "He loves you."

Claudia sighed. "I know, but I want him to act like it." She sighed again and then perked up, straightening her spine. "I'm sure you have work to do, so I'll leave you alone now. I certainly have work to do. See ya later."

Audra sat in her chair and turned on her computer, except she couldn't concentrate. The scent of the flowers filled the small space of her cubicle and posed a fragrant distraction. Unable to resist, she pressed her nose to the bouquet and inhaled their scent.

She looked at the card again. Should she send a message through Claudia?

No. Shaking her head, she tucked the card into a pocket of her purse.

From what she had seen online, Damon could have any woman he wanted, and she'd noticed how they panted after him at the party, their attention palpable. Women came effortlessly to him.

She still wasn't sure what she wanted to do but decided not to give in so easily. Damon Foster was going to have to work for her attention, and that would let her know how serious he was.

* * *

The flowers didn't stop coming.

Two to three times a week, Audra received a surprise at work—flowers or some little gift. The flower arrangements were always different, and the gifts weren't extravagant but thoughtful. He sent gourmet treats, like artisan chocolates and rich, delicious cheesecake, which she shared with Claudia. He also sent a plant that she placed on her desk. Her absolute favorite present was a puzzle with a picture of him. She thought that was hilarious.

The man was hot, rich, and had a great sense of humor. He was definitely dangerous. She understood why women flocked to him.

She began to look forward to the deliveries and idly wondered, *How long did he plan to keep sending her gifts?*

Chapter Five

Damon didn't have a game tonight, but he'd had to practice and watch film and barely made it home in time to shower, change, and arrive at Audra's workplace at the end of the day. He didn't want to draw attention to himself and tugged his cap lower on his forehead, hoping not to be recognized.

He watched the employees pouring out the front doors of the building. Then he saw her, looking professional yet sexy in a white blouse and black sarong skirt that showed off her figure. She carried the bouquet of roses he had sent earlier in the day, so she was easy to spot. Her hair was pulled into a ponytail that swayed with each step she took in a pair of black heels.

"Damn," he muttered, licking his lips.

This wasn't the first time he'd seen her since the party. He'd stopped by once before and sat in his car, watching as she exited the building. He'd had the same visceral reaction and muttered the same word—*Damn*.

Pushing away from his black SUV, he shoved his hands in his pockets.

Audra looked both ways and then crossed the street. When she arrived on his side, she veered right, probably toward her car. She hadn't seen him.

"Audra." He took several steps as she looked over her shoulder. She paused, her eyes lighting up and a faint smile touching her lips. A good sign.

Damon stayed put, not wanting to freak her out.

"Damon." She said his name with surprise and wonder.

"Hi. I swear I'm not a stalker."

"Says the man standing outside my job."

He laughed. "You have a good sense of humor."

"I like to think I'm funny."

His eyes dropped to her full, ruby-colored lips before returning to her dark eyes. "Can we talk?"

"Sure." Clutching the roses in her hands, she slowly approached and stopped directly in front of him.

"I see you received the flowers."

"I've received all your flowers. And the gifts. Did you get my message?"

She had sent a message through Claudia, who passed it on to Jacob, thanking Damon for the gifts. She hadn't provided her phone number, though, which was what he'd been hoping for.

"I did, which is why I'm here." He tilted his head sideways. "Have I made any headway?"

She copied his move by cocking her head and shifting her lips into a moue. "Should I be worried about you?"

"What do you mean?" Damon asked.

"You've been sending me gifts for the past three weeks, and now you're waiting outside my job."

"That's a fair point, but I promise I'm not dangerous."

"Are you sure about that?" she asked.

He chuckled. "We should probably start over, or I need to start over. Honestly, I don't usually act like this about women."

"Let me guess, I'm 'different?'" She did air quotes with one hand.

"Come on now, don't do that."

"Don't do what?" she asked with wide-eyed innocence.

"What you did two seconds ago. Basically, whatever I say, you won't believe me, right?"

"Everything you're about to say, I've heard before."

He narrowed his eyes. "You're a beautiful woman, and you've probably heard a lot of bullshit from other men, but I'm not like—"

"Other men," she finished.

He paused. "That's not a line."

"Of course not," she said.

Damon let out a little laugh, shaking his head as he bit his bottom lip. "Why did you send the message to me?"

"Because I appreciate all the gifts."

"And why do you think I'm sending you gifts?"

She shrugged.

"Audra, if I wasn't interested in you, do you think I would be trying this hard? I admit it, okay? I'm obsessed. Maybe a little stalkerish, but I'm harmless. I want to get to know you. Let me take you out. One night, that's all. We don't have to call it a date. We can call it two acquaintances getting to know each other. Two buddies going out to dinner."

"Hmm..."

"Come on, we'll be bros. Except one of us is shaped like a Coke bottle, has beautiful brown eyes, and lips that haunt my dreams." His voice dipped lower at the end.

She swallowed and lowered her gaze. "Now you're making me blush."

Do or die time.

Damon stepped closer, and she looked up at him. "I would like to get to know you better, but if you're not interested—and you want me to stop—I'll stop now. I don't want you to feel uncomfortable, and it's not my style to push up on a woman who's not checking for me. You say stop, and I'll go away. You'll never hear from me again."

He held his breath, abs tight as he waited for her reply.

She averted her gaze for a moment, as if in deep thought. "You seem like a decent guy, Damon."

He heard the "but" coming, and the corrosive ache of disappointment seared his chest.

She licked her lips. "I would like to take you up on your offer for dinner."

Damon was so surprised by her answer, at first he didn't respond. Then he shook off his stupor. "Okay."

"We're going as friends, right? Buddies?" Audra asked.

"That's right. Completely platonic. I'll treat you like one of the guys," Damon confirmed. *Yeah, right.*

"Good, because I wouldn't want there to be any misunderstandings. You seem to have a lot of women that occupy your time, so..."

"You looked me up online."

"Of course. You have quite the roster, and I'm not talking about baseball."

He briefly closed his eyes and groaned. "My dating situation is not as bad as you think. Sometimes celebrities link up for publicity purposes. I promise you, you don't have anything to worry about. I don't have a girlfriend, and your girl Claudia said you're not seeing anyone seriously."

"I'm not," she confirmed.

Perfect. "Then we can both go out and have a nice meal and enjoy each other's company."

"As friends."

"Oh yeah, as friends."

"Sounds good." She smiled, and she was so damn beautiful his chest hurt.

Before she could change her mind, Damon made sure they exchanged numbers and then walked her to her royal blue BMW.

"Are you busy this weekend? I have a couple of ideas for restaurants," Damon said. Now that she'd agreed to go out with him, he wanted to lock her into a date.

Audra stopped at her driver's side door. "This weekend works for me, but I have a request."

"Shoot."

"Although I didn't know it initially, you're obviously very famous. I'd like to go somewhere low-key, if that's okay with you. I don't want my photo all over the gossip blogs and social media."

Damon understood her reservations. The blogs could be vicious. When they weren't dissecting his love life, they were scrutinizing the women he dated—everything from their hair-styles to the shoes on their feet. Most of the women he became involved with were accustomed to the attention, and some welcomed it because of their line of work as actresses or models. Someone like Audra wasn't used to having the eyes of the public on her and clearly wanted to maintain her privacy.

"That's not a problem," he assured her. "Matter of fact, one of the places I'm thinking about would be perfect. We can arrive separately and meet up inside. Does that work for you?"

She seemed surprised by his accommodating suggestion. "Sounds perfect."

"Good. I'll make the reservation and call you with the details later."

"You'll make the reservation? I figured you'd have a personal assistant who takes care of those types of tasks for you. Someone who orders these flowers every week too."

"Is that what you think?"

"It's pretty normal."

"Maybe, and I'm not saying that I don't have an assistant. I do. He takes care of a lot of stuff for me, but I order those flowers for you every week, I pick the gifts, and I'm going to handle our dinner reservations."

"Oh. I didn't know." She seemed genuinely surprised, a soft wrinkle appearing on her forehead. Before she climbed into her car, she turned one more time to face him. "Why?"

"Why what?"

"Why do you handle those tasks yourself if you have someone who can do them for you?"

"Because I want to. You deserve the personal touch."

If her skin had been lighter, he was certain he would see her cheeks turn red. Instead, she lowered her gaze, and a soft smile touched her lips.

"You're something else, Damon. I look forward to getting your call."

Chapter Six

Damon had called, and tonight was the night.

Audra checked her appearance in the bathroom mirror. Black slacks and a purple top, her hair in large curls that rested like dark clouds on her shoulders.

Am I showing too much cleavage?

No, she decided. Considering some of the clothing she'd seen women wearing in the photos with Damon, this outfit was pretty demure.

She turned out the light and went into the bedroom. Kerilyn was lying on her stomach on the bed, playing a video game on an old phone Audra had given her.

Audra picked up her purse. "How does Mommy look?" She turned in a slow circle.

Her daughter's eyes brightened. "Pretty! Are you going on a date?"

"I'm going out with a friend." Audra tucked the purse under her arm. For the most part, she didn't share her romantic life with her daughter and had never introduced her to any other man.

Kerilyn sat up. "Is it a boy or a girl?"

"It's a boy, but boys and girls can be friends," Audra patiently explained.

"Are you going to kiss him?"

"Kerilyn!"

Her daughter giggled.

"I'm going to kiss you!" Audra smothered her face with kisses, enjoying the sound of her daughter's laughter as she wriggled in her arms, pretending to want to get away.

Finally, she looked down at her. "I'm going to leave in a few minutes. Be good for Grandma and *Abuelo*."

"I'm *always* good." Kerilyn hopped off the bed. "Can I have ice cream later?"

"You can, but not too late, okay?"

"Okay."

"Bye-bye. Love you." Audra bent down and gave her daughter one last kiss.

"Bye-bye. Have fun!" Kerilyn raced off toward her grand-parents' bedroom.

Audra took a deep breath. She hadn't been on a date in a while, and Damon made her incredibly nervous.

She descended the stairs to the first floor and climbed into the car she had hired for the night. She greeted the chauffeur, an older man with graying hair, before sliding onto the backseat.

As the driver headed down the driveway, she did another check of her appearance in her compact. "You look fine," she muttered to herself.

"Excuse me, ma'am?" the driver said, meeting her eyes in the rearview mirror.

"Nothing. I'm talking to myself," Audra said with an embarrassed laugh.

Damon had chosen the restaurant Prime Table, a small,

intimate establishment known for its steaks and lobster mac and cheese. Audra was surprised he had been able to get a reservation on such short notice. She had only been there once and was looking forward to visiting again.

When she arrived, she gave her name at the front, and the hostess escorted her toward the rear of the building where Damon was waiting. He came to his feet as she approached, and her eyes absorbed every inch of him.

He looked delicious in a dark plaid sport coat paired with a light-colored shirt and dark pants. The fit of his clothes was perfect, emphasizing his broad shoulders and physique. With his hair and beard freshly trimmed, it was hard to keep her eyes off him.

He seemed to be having a similar problem, casting an appreciative gaze down the length of her body. "You look amazing." His voice was as smooth and rich as melted caramel and made between her thighs quiver with longing.

As Audra lowered into her chair, Damon stepped behind her and gently pushed it in place.

"Thank you," she said over her shoulder, catching the appealing scent of his aftershave.

He returned to his chair, and she folded her hands in her lap. *Calm down*, she chided herself. She was way too excited and aroused.

Since she and Kerilyn's father split, she'd been on dates, but nothing serious. Spending time with Damon caused nervous energy to spike inside her. Tonight with him felt more momentous—for lack of a better word—than the dates she had been on since her breakup.

"This arrangement was a bit odd for me," Damon said.

"What do you mean?"

"Having to meet you here. I'm used to picking up a woman or, at the very least, sending a car for her."

"You're a very popular man, and as I explained, I'd rather not show up in one of those online articles about you. I have family members who are famous and semi-famous, and I'm familiar with how misinformation can circulate about celebrities and those close to them."

"I understand that you don't want that to happen to you."

"I definitely don't."

The waitress arrived to take their drink orders and then left them alone again. Damon sat back and watched Audra with undisguised interest, his eyes practically boring into her soul. "What kind of misinformation do you think would crop up about us?"

She shrugged. "We're here as friends, right? But I'm sure if people saw us together, they'd make assumptions."

"Such as?" he prompted.

"They might assume we're a couple and that we're... you know."

"Sleeping together," he supplied.

"Yes."

"And we're not yet," Damon said.

"Exactly. We're—" She stopped abruptly. "*Yet?*"

"Did I say yet?" he asked, looking unrepentant.

"The innocent act doesn't work for you. Yes, you said yet."

Damon leaned toward her, and she held her breath.

"How about we both stop pretending? You know I'm not interested in being your friend. I've never sent flowers to my friends or drooled when I saw them approach me in the restaurant where we're having dinner. Let's see how the evening goes. Because the last thing I want to do is be your friend, Audra, but if I told you what I really wanted, I might scare you off. And I don't want to scare you off." He started studying the open menu. "You've been here before. What do you recommend?"

He switched gears so abruptly, she almost thought she had

imagined his intensity, but there was no imagining the breathlessness she experienced from his bold words.

Audra resettled in her chair. She could handle the change. "I, er, I had the ribeye last time with the lobster mac and cheese and broccolini."

"Good?" Damon arched an eyebrow at her.

"Excellent. I think I'll get that again." She scanned the menu, in case there was something else she might want.

"I'll get that too." He closed his menu.

"No, we have to order different meals. At least order a different side. That way we can—" She caught herself. She was being way too familiar with him and making assumptions. He might not like to share his food.

"What?" Damon prompted.

"Nothing."

"You want to order different sides so we can try each other's food. Am I right?"

"Well..."

"I like that idea. I'll order the mashed potato soufflé and the orange carrots. How about that?"

"You should get what you want," Audra said.

"That is what I want. I was taking the easy way out because you confirmed those other dishes were good. This way we can try different things. Okay?"

She smiled. "Okay."

The waitress returned with their drinks, and they placed their orders, and Damon included an order of stuffed mushrooms.

Audra took a sip of her red wine. "Mmm. Good. How's your rum and Coke?"

"Strong. I think it's rum, rum, and Coke."

She laughed. "So tell me about yourself. I know you're from Arkansas. Does your family still live there?"

"Yes, my parents still live there. I don't have any siblings—" He broke off when her phone rang.

Audra checked the screen. "This is my mother. Excuse me." She put the phone to her ear. "Hi, Mom. Is everything okay?" Her mother knew she was out with a man, so the reason for the call must be important.

"Honey, I'm sorry. I didn't want to call you, but Kerilyn has been agitated for the past fifteen minutes. She ate a big bowl of ice cream and says she's sleepy but refuses to go to bed without her pink blanket, and I can't find it."

"Mommy, where's my blanket?" Audra heard her daughter's distressed voice in the background. She sounded like she was in the midst of a full-blown panic attack.

"I don't know why she's so attached to that thing," Audra told her mother. "It's in the hamper. She spilled apple juice on it. There's another blanket—the yellow one with the blue rabbits on it. She likes that one almost as much and should fall asleep if you cover her with it."

"Oh yes, the yellow blanket. Okay, I'll look for it."

"It should be in the bottom drawer on the right of her dresser. I'll hold while you check."

"Honey, you don't have to do that."

"I don't mind." Audra shot a quick glance at Damon, who was politely averting his eyes and pretending not to listen.

"One second."

She could tell her mother was moving through the house.

"Are you enjoying yourself?" Rose asked.

"Yes," Audra replied, keeping her voice neutral.

"Found it!" Relief flooded her mother's voice.

Kerilyn's dramatic moans stopped, replaced by a squeal of happiness.

"You should see her little face," Rose said.

"Sounds like she stopped whining."

"She did. Thanks, honey. I won't bother you again."

"It's no bother, Mom. Talk to you later." Audra hung up and shot an apologetic smile at Damon. "Sorry about that. I have a daughter." He didn't blink or react to that declaration, so she continued. "My mother called—well, you heard. My daughter, Kerilyn, insisted on having her very special blanket before she would go to bed. The only time the blanket doesn't matter is when she sleeps in my bed."

"No need to apologize."

Audra smoothed her palms over the cloth napkin across her thighs. "Don't take this the wrong way, but you're a lot nicer than I expected."

His eyes narrowed in amusement. "Really? What did you expect?"

"I thought you'd be kind of... arrogant. Cocky."

"I'm both of those things."

She laughed out loud. "Well, you're also a gentleman, polite, and easy to get along with—so far."

He continued to watch her.

"You're staring," Audra said.

"I can't help it. I like looking at you. Your eyes light up when you smile or laugh. It's very attractive."

Warmth heated her cheeks. "Are you going to pay me compliments all night?"

A slow smile took over his lips. "If you let me."

Chapter Seven

"We were talking about you before the phone call, weren't we? So you're an only child?" Audra asked.

Damon nodded. "Yes."

"Did you always play baseball, or were you interested in other sports?"

"I played other sports but excelled at baseball. Nowadays, it consumes my life, but that's normal for someone playing sports at a professional level. When we're not playing, we're training or preparing by watching film. We also have to be careful about our diet."

"But you love it."

"I can't imagine doing anything else."

"When you're not training or playing, what do you do?"

"Well, I've been working on some business ventures and ideas for life after baseball. In my downtime, I try to do some mentoring, but I'm not able to do it as much as I'd like. In between all those things, I sometimes squeeze in time to pursue a woman who interests me."

"I see. Making time for the important issues."

"Of course." Amusement filled his eyes.

"By the way, I never verbally, out my mouth, thanked you for the flowers and the gifts—so, thank you. Each delivery brightened my day."

"Good to hear."

"I especially liked the puzzle made out of a photo of you."

He let out a throaty laugh. "You liked that, huh?"

"It was a top-notch gift."

"It's one of a kind. You're the only person in the world who has one."

She liked his sense of humor. "I figured so."

"Have you tried to put it together yet?"

"Not yet, but I've put it on my to-do list."

"I'm going to check in with you to see if you've done it," Damon warned.

"Darn, I shouldn't have told you my plans. Now there's so much pressure." Audra sipped her wine, thoroughly amused by their conversation.

Damon swirled his drink. "Tell me something I don't know about you."

"What do you want to know?"

"Anything. What makes Audra Connor tick? What's important to you?" His eyes remained on her.

"Those are interesting questions. I'll tackle the second question first and say my family is important to me. As I mentioned, I have a little girl. She's very smart. I know every parent says that, but the other day she showed me how to change a setting on my phone, and she's a whiz with the iPad. She always tries to stay up later than her bedtime, and she can sometimes convince my mother to let her—we live with my parents—stay up and have ice cream and cake and whatever

41

else her heart desires. Being the first grandchild has its privileges."

He laughed softly. "I bet."

"I'm going on and on." Audra twisted the napkin in her lap. She was more out of practice than she realized. What man wanted to hear about a woman's kid on their first date—or whatever this was?

Damon sat forward and rested his hand on the table, his expression earnest. "It's fine. Matter of fact, I'm glad you're sharing stories about your daughter. Gives me insight into your relationship."

Audra smiled appreciatively. "She's the center of my universe," she said honestly.

He nodded, as if that declaration had revealed something to him. "You have siblings?"

"Oh yes," she said emphatically, followed by a laugh.

He arched an eyebrow. "What does that answer mean?"

"I come from a big family. Blended, actually. There are seven kids, plus my parents—so a family of nine."

His eyebrows shifted higher. "You weren't kidding when you said big."

"No, and—"

The waitress arrived and placed a sizzling dish of stuffed mushrooms in front of them.

After she left, both Damon and Audra placed one on their plates. Audra was the first to try it and hummed her satisfaction.

"Yeah?" Damon said.

"Really good." She watched as he placed the appetizer in his mouth and then raised his eyebrows, clearly impressed.

"You know what? I think I'm gonna finish this on my own." He pulled the dish toward him, and Audra grabbed his wrist.

"Hey! I want more too." She dragged the dish back to the middle of the table.

He chuckled. "I guess I shouldn't come between you and your food."

"Never ever," she advised, scooping out another mushroom and shooting him a mock angry look.

He grinned. "Okay, so finish telling me about your big blended family. Explain the dynamics of it."

Audra finished chewing her bite. "My mother had three kids—me, my sister, and my older brother—when she met my stepfather, Benicio. He's Mexican and had three boys of his own. Then they had a child together, a boy, the one we call the baby."

"He's number seven."

"Exactly."

"So, two girls and five boys."

"Yes, and the boys were nightmares sometimes. They terrorized us."

"But I bet no one ever messed with you."

"Absolutely not. They could terrorize us, but no one else was allowed to. To this day, they're very protective."

"It would be nice to have a big family," Damon said, a note of wistfulness in his voice.

"Being an only child, I understand why you would say that, but trust me—it wasn't all fun and games." Audra sliced a particularly large mushroom in half.

"I bet it wasn't with seven kids. I'm sure there was plenty of chaos."

"Mostly when we were younger," Audra admitted. "Imagine blending not only families but cultures and having to deal with language barriers. It was... interesting at first. We had a housekeeper and a chef, but my mother learned to cook Mexican dishes. Then they had their own traditions for the holidays, which were different from ours. They're Catholic, we were raised Baptist. You get the picture. Eventually, we started gelling, and you couldn't convince me that my Mexican brothers are not kin."

"That's the way it should be. Family isn't defined by blood. Family is in the connections we make and the bonds we build with people in our lives."

He spoke with a fervency that caught Audra's attention.

"Sounds like you know a little bit about that," she commented.

For the first time, the smile on his lips seemed forced. "Long, ugly story. One of these days, I'll tell you about it."

"I guess that means I better stick around."

"I guess so."

Chapter Eight

After their delicious meal, Damon didn't want the night to end. He wanted to prolong his time with Audra and invited her to go for a walk. Thankfully, she said yes.

He grabbed an unmarked cap and sunglasses from his vehicle—a "disguise" he kept for when he wanted to go incognito. He pulled the cap low on his forehead before they set off down the sidewalk.

They walked in comfortable silence for a while. Occasionally, cars passed by, and every now and again a pedestrian approached, nodding a greeting as they walked by.

"Do you miss being anonymous?" Audra asked.

"Sometimes," Damon admitted. "But then I remember how blessed I am. I mean, I get to play baseball, a sport I took up when I was a kid—and make a ton of money doing it. Being recognizable is a small price to pay for the privilege, and most times it's not too bad. Like right now, no one expects to see me walking down the street, so even if they recognize me under this cap and behind these sunglasses, they'll think they made a mistake." He paused. "The worst part isn't the fans, although they can sometimes become outrageous."

"Outrageous how?"

"Doing anything to meet me, which includes hiding in my hotel room or something else crazy."

"My brother Ignacio is an actor, and as he becomes more famous, the stories become more outrageous, so I know what you mean. My father was an actor too, and boy, does he have tales to tell!"

"You understand where I'm coming from."

"I do," Audra said with a nod. "So what's the worst part?"

"The media, or what they call media nowadays. Every person with a camera and a mic is a journalist now, and the real journalists have become sensationalists to keep up. Stories from anonymous sources, hearsay, and plain old gossip about shit they don't know."

"Jumping to conclusions without the facts," Audra said.

"Exactly. Shit is exhausting sometimes. Mostly I ignore the stories, unless it's something so bad I need to get my PR team involved. Other times, we use them, creating our own publicity for whatever we want."

"Sounds sneaky."

He shrugged. "I call it making lemons out of lemonade."

As they continued walking and talking, Damon realized he was very relaxed. Being with Audra was low pressure. He didn't feel the need to perform and didn't have to be "The Flash," the way he did with other women. He could simply be Damon.

Every now and again, their arms brushed, and awareness seeped through his shirtsleeves and rippled over his skin. He wondered if she experienced the same sensation.

"I have a question for you," he said.

"Okay." She dragged out the word, sounding cautious.

"Don't sound so worried. It's a simple question. You dissed my house when you were there, so—"

"I didn't diss your house," she said, sounding appalled.

"You said it was colorless and cold. Is that a compliment?"

"I mean..."

"That's what I thought. So, you dissed my house," Damon continued. "What would you change?"

"Are you asking me for decorating tips?"

"A little. I don't know anything about decorating. I thought about hiring someone to help me, but I figured I could do okay on my own. I'm kinda frugal. We didn't have much when I was growing up, and I know I won't play ball forever. Hell, I could get injured this year, and my career could end, so I'm really careful with my money."

"Which means you want me to help you for free?"

"Yes," he confirmed.

She laughed—and once again, he was smitten by her beauty when she did. The tightness in his chest—an unfamiliar stirring —suggested he felt more than attraction, but he didn't want to delve too deeply into his innermost thoughts at the moment.

"Your place isn't bad, but you definitely need more color and different textures. Everything is hard and white."

"I was going for a clean, finished look."

"You can still achieve that with a few changes. What you have now could be the baseline, and then you layer in the changes." She spoke with her hands as she explained. "That's my opinion."

"Okay," Damon said, nodding.

"I'll text you some suggestions and examples of pillows and furnishings you can add. They'll be nice pieces that aren't expensive. Nothing drastic—if you're really open to change."

"I am, and that would be great. Thanks." He saw this as a good sign that she was interested in communicating with him in the future, and if her voice was any indication, she seemed excited about pulling together items for him.

They approached the restaurant again, and Damon felt disappointment trickle through him. They came to a stop near the door. "If you like, I can drop you at home instead of you having to call another car," he suggested.

She gazed up at him. "I don't want to inconvenience you. I live far from here, south of the city."

"I don't mind at all. Besides, it'll give us a chance to talk some more about how you can improve the decor in my condo. Now there's a word I never thought I'd hear myself say—*decor*."

One of her pretty smiles lit up her face. "If you don't mind, I don't mind."

"Right this way." He extended his arm, and she took it.

He escorted her to his SUV and helped her climb into the passenger side. He went around to the driver's side, removed his hat and sunglasses, and placed them in the back.

On the ride to her house, they talked more about their work lives. He told her about baseball, though it was obvious she knew very little. She told him about the work she did at her stepfather's company as an administrative assistant. She mentioned wanting to move up in the company, but he suspected her heart wasn't in it. She didn't become animated the way she did when she talked about changing the decor of his place.

She also talked more about her family and her daughter. She never once mentioned her daughter's father, though. Was he in the picture, and how much of a problem would he be if he was?

They both fell silent as he took the long, tree-lined driveway toward the impressive mansion she called home. Her parents' money was obviously long.

He parked in front of the stairs leading to the double front doors. "Home sweet home," he announced.

After he helped her down from the SUV, they slowly climbed the stairs.

Audra took a deep breath. "Well, I had a really nice time tonight. Thank you for a delicious dinner."

"And great conversation," Damon added.

She laughed briefly. She seemed nervous all of a sudden, which he thought was adorable. She was like a breath of fresh air, with no agenda.

"I enjoyed the conversation too," she admitted.

Damon looked around the property. "This place is huge. I feel like you're out of my league."

"Believe me, I'm not. This all belongs to my parents, and I just live here for the time being. My father built this place to accommodate all of us." She cleared her throat. "So, I—"

"Audra, I want to see you again." He looked into her eyes so she'd know he was serious.

"As friends?" she asked in a teasing tone.

Damon didn't smile. "Nah. More than friends."

She opened her mouth to speak, but he cut her off. "I know you think my lifestyle is a bit intimidating, and I understand. Being in the public eye definitely has its drawbacks, but no one has to know about us right now. We can keep things low-key, get to know each other without all eyes being on us. Unless..."

"Unless what?" she prompted.

"You and Kerilyn's dad are still..."

Her eyes widened, and she shook her head so vehemently her hair fell across her face. "No. Absolutely not."

She was so adamant, he almost laughed. Damn. Her ex must be a real jerk.

"Okay, so I don't have to worry about him."

"He and I are done and have been for years. His name is

Kerry. Yes, I named my daughter after him." She rolled her eyes in disgust at her own decision-making. "Anyway, let me repeat —he and I are done."

Damon stepped closer. "In that case, we can see each other again."

She frowned slightly. "You can have any woman you want," she said, sounding perplexed.

"Except you?"

Uncertainty flickered in her eyes. "I'm not looking for a serious relationship right now, and I know you aren't either—obviously."

"Obviously?"

"You're a serial dater. You don't stick to one woman very long, and there's nothing wrong with that," she added hastily. "I enjoyed myself with you, but I have to be honest. I'm not sure dating you would be a wise decision, and I make terrible decisions."

He didn't particularly like her assessment of his dating life, but she was right about one thing—a serious relationship wasn't in the cards for him right now. He was young and rich, and though he did want to spend more time with Audra, he didn't know how long his interest would last and didn't want to make her any promises he might break.

She wasn't like some of the other women he dated. She didn't seem like the type looking to get pregnant and be set for the next eighteen years. Nor was she an up-and-coming celebrity or model seeking free publicity by being on his arm. From everything he'd learned about her tonight, she seemed like a regular person, and right now, he wanted regular. He craved it in a way he never thought he would.

"We can take things slow if you like. I enjoyed myself tonight, and you enjoyed yourself. We can kick it and see where things go."

"Just kick it, huh?" Audra said, uncertainty remaining in her expression.

Damon took her hand and gazed into her eyes. "You have to at least help me decorate my place, right? Might as well get the perks of dating me too. What do you think...?"

"You're persistent, I'll give you that," Audra said with a short laugh.

"Does that mean I'll see you again, Audra?" He held his breath, his belly oddly tight with the stress of worrying that she'd answer no.

Finally, she smiled. "Yes. I look forward to it."

He grinned. He wanted to pull her into a kiss but suspected that would be too much for her at the moment. He carefully brushed her hair away from her face, and for a moment, his eyes dipped to her upturned lips. Full, lush, temptingly red.

Using monumental self-control, he kissed her cheek instead. Her skin was soft, and she smelled like heaven. Biting back a groan of hunger, he stepped back.

Audra seemed surprised.

"Good night," he said.

"Good night, and thank you for a great evening." She studied him for a moment, as if trying to figure him out. Then she disappeared inside the house.

Grinning, Damon jogged down the steps and climbed into his SUV.

Chapter Nine

Damon didn't have a game tonight, but he was on his way to the gym to work out. After he merged into traffic, he dialed his father's number in Arkansas.

Chadwick Foster tended to rise early, sitting out on the back porch as he sipped his coffee, so Damon wasn't surprised when he answered at this hour.

"Hey, Pop, how's it goin'?"

"Hey, son. Going all right out here. How's your shoulder?"

Damon rotated his right shoulder, which had suffered a minor injury weeks ago during spring training.

"Much better. I'm headed to the gym now to work out. Where's Ma?"

"She left the house early today. You remember Joanna from down the street? Her husband died, so your mom has been keeping her company and helping her out since she doesn't have any family living close by. They have an appointment at the funeral home this morning."

That didn't surprise Damon. His mother was that kind of

woman—very caring and in tune with other people. No surprise, since she had been a social worker for years.

"What can I help you with?" Chadwick asked.

"What makes you think I need help with something?" Damon replied.

"You have that sound in your voice."

He chuckled softly. His father knew him well. "You're right. It's about a woman."

"Uh-oh."

"It's not bad. I met someone, and I really like her. Real talk, I'm obsessed with her." He gave his father a quick explanation of how he met Audra, the flowers and gifts, and their first date a couple of days ago.

"I think she had a good time, but before she agreed to go out with me, she treated me like a regular dude and took a long time to give me a shot. She probably wouldn't have if I didn't go up to her job. That's why I have my doubts. I want to call her, but I don't want to come across as a stalker."

"Too late," his father quipped.

"Damn."

Chadwick chuckled. "Let me see if I understand what you're saying. You went on a date and had a good time, but now you're worried about calling her too soon. Do I have that right?"

"Yes." He never had this problem with other women he dated. They understood he was seeing multiple women at the same time, and they were happy when he called. He knew he couldn't treat Audra the same way, but at the same time he didn't quite know how to move with her.

He'd been an athletic star since middle school and was used to being catered to—by women, teachers, fellow students, and adults. This was the first time he had to put in the work and didn't want to mess things up.

"Have you communicated with her at all since the date?" his father asked.

Damon checked his side mirror and switched lanes. "I sent a text after I dropped her off on Saturday night. That's it. Nothing since then."

"So you put in all that effort to win her over, and now that you've got her, you're pulling back. Do I have that correct?"

"When you put it that way..."

"That's not me. That's how this young lady will see your lack of communication, son. Now she's probably thinking you didn't have a good time or were somehow disappointed by the date. She probably thinks you're no longer interested."

He had never considered that angle. "I don't want her to think that I didn't have a good time, but it's only been a couple of days. I don't want to be too pushy."

"But you're interested?"

"Hell, yeah."

"Well then, it's time to let her know. Talk to the young lady. Make plans for another date. If she's not interested, she'll let you know. Then you can move on."

Move on. Those words sounded so final. "I don't know if I could."

"What do you mean?"

He'd thought long and hard about his feelings for Audra, and only one answer made sense. "I think Audra Connor is my future wife."

There was silence on the other end for several moments.

"I've never heard you talk like that before," his father finally said.

Damon enjoyed the women he spent time with—models, actresses, female athletes, unknowns. Yet no one had captured his interest the way that she did.

"There's something about her."

54

"Well then you better hurry up and call her, because if she's that amazing, someone else is going to swoop her up."

"I'm not letting that happen," Damon said with determination.

"She must be something."

"She is. She has the best laugh, a beautiful smile, and a great sense of humor. She's fine as hell, and the fact that she doesn't care about my career or who I am is kind of nice, you know?"

"I know what you mean. I experienced the same with your mother," Chadwick said, his voice sounding wistful. "It's like coming home."

Warmth filled Damon's chest. "Yeah. That's the feeling. Like I'm home. Safe." He swallowed. That word—*safe*—had slipped from his lips unexpectedly.

"You doing okay otherwise?" Chadwick asked in a gentle voice.

"Yeah, yeah, I'm cool. Just dealing with the usual stuff on the field and off. Audra's a temporary distraction."

"Good to hear."

For a moment, awkward silence hovered between them like a dark cloud before a rainstorm. Damon knew his father wanted to say more but probably wouldn't because he knew Damon didn't want to hear it. The nightmares from the abuse had stopped years ago, but the memories lingered. Unfortunately, he would never fully be free of them. He couldn't control his thoughts, but he could control whether or not he gave those painful moments any space in conversations with his loved ones.

"Listen, I better go. Thanks for the talk, Pop."

"Any time, son. Take care."

After he hung up, the pressure in Damon's chest eased. He cursed under his breath, hating that he continued to have such an adverse reaction to what had happened to him as a kid.

But life was better now. Much better.

His mind shifted to Audra, and like the sun peeking through the clouds, the memory of her radiant smile pushed aside the last trace of his pain. He breathed easier.

He'd give her a call today. He'd gone long enough without hearing her voice.

*　*　*

Today hadn't been the best day for Audra. Several times she'd caught herself doodling distractedly on her notepad.

Except for a short *Good night* text, she hadn't heard from Damon since Saturday. In the meantime, he'd taken over her mind. As she typed a memo at her desk, she kept seeing his white-toothed smile against milk chocolate skin. She heard his deep-throated, sexy male laugh and felt the tingles from the intense way he studied her, as if he hung on every word she spoke.

He hadn't even kissed her—well, not a real kiss—but she still felt his soft lips on her skin and the brush of his beard against her cheek.

Why didn't he kiss her properly!

That's what she had been expecting when he gazed down at her, and that's all she could think about now: kissing him. She knew he'd be a good kisser too. With lips like that and all that swagger, no way that man wouldn't deliver.

With a loud sigh, Audra pushed away from her desk and went to copy a document. She placed the duplicates in an interoffice envelope and dropped them in the outgoing mailbox near the door.

Back at her desk, she sank into her seat and stared at the report on her computer screen. Maybe he didn't enjoy himself.

Audra buried her face in her hands. *Get back to work!* she screamed inside her head. And that's what she did, forcing Damon from her mind and concentrating solely on the work at hand to preoccupy herself.

After lunch, she had a quick meeting and then returned to her desk to see a missed call on the phone in her drawer.

Damon.

She gasped, her pulse jumping erratically. He'd followed up the call with a text.

> Hey there, hope you aren't ignoring me. I called to see if ur free on Saturday night. If not, clear your schedule. I'm taking you out again.

Biting her bottom lip, Audra replied.

> Was that a question or a demand?

A minute later, he responded.

> Which one would have you saying yes?

> Honestly, either.

> Good to know. So you're free?

> Yes.

> I'll pick you up at 7:15 for dinner. Casual dress. Comfortable shoes. We'll be doing a little walking after our meal.

I'll be ready.

"What are you smiling about?" Claudia stood beside Audra with a hand on one hip. Her blonde hair was styled in a single braid that rested over one shoulder.

"I have another date," Audra said. She had been worried she wouldn't hear from Damon and couldn't stop cheesing because she had.

"Is it with the person I think it's with? Mr. Foster of the Atlanta Braves?" Claudia asked.

"Yes, it's him."

Claudia let out a quiet squeal, and Audra joined her.

"Aren't you glad you came with me to that party?"

"I was already glad because I had a good time. Now I'm doubly glad," Audra admitted.

"Keep me posted."

Claudia sauntered off, and Audra sat at her desk, staring at the messages exchanged between her and Damon.

Saturday was too far away.

Chapter Ten

"The Aquarium?" Audra exclaimed, eyes wide as the chauffeur pulled up to the building.

When Damon had told her to dress casually and wear comfortable shoes, she had silently worried about what that meant but was open to new adventures. Anticipating an outdoor activity, she wore black jeans, a floral, loose-fitting top, and wedge heels.

This, however, was a surprise.

The Georgia Aquarium was an animal sanctuary of more than 600,000 square feet and contained more than eleven million gallons of water. She hadn't visited in two years, when she had been a chaperone for her daughter's preschool class trip.

"This ain't no regular schmegular trip to the Aquarium. You're about to get the VIP access tour." Standing outside the car, Damon extended a hand and helped her out.

"Oooh, VIP? I can't wait."

They had stayed in touch the entire week and talked almost every day on the phone—even when he was out of town. She loved hearing his voice and discussing everything under the sun, which made her feel closer to him, as if they'd known each other for years.

She had also sent him suggestions on how to improve his home, and he liked the ideas, promising he would order the items right away.

Hand in hand, they walked to a side door, which was opened from the inside by a uniformed guide. The young man —who looked a few years younger than Audra—greeted them with a cheery "Welcome!" and ushered them inside.

Deliciously overwhelmed, she felt like a princess walking through the empty aquarium after hours. The interior was dimly lit, the large tanks filled with water and emitting soothing light in shades of blue and green.

The guide led them to a table covered with a crisp white tablecloth.

"This is nice," Audra breathed, taking in the shimmering light from the tank beside them and the colorful fish darting through the water.

Damon picked up the bouquet of flowers from the table and presented them to her. He was comfortably dressed in high-end black deerskin sneakers, a short-sleeved navy Henley, and khaki slacks.

Audra pressed her nose to the flower petals and inhaled their perfumed scent. "What is all this for?" she whispered.

"I want tonight to be unforgettable, so the next time I ask you out, you don't hesitate."

"I didn't hesitate when you asked me out."

"Yeah, you did. You took way too long to respond to my text."

"Because I wasn't by my phone when you texted," Audra explained. She couldn't remember anyone ever going to this much trouble for her before. Even more impressive was that he'd planned the entire night without her input. "I don't know what to say. Who raised you, Casanova and Cupid?"

Damon chuckled and pulled out her chair. "I'm going to assume that means I'm doing a good job."

"You are. I feel very special." She settled into the seat and placed the flowers on the table. "I don't know a single person who can say they had dinner with sharks and fish watching."

"Now you'll be the one to tell that story." His brown eyes sparkled across the table at her. He appeared as excited to unveil the evening as she was to experience it.

The guide left and was replaced by a server, a woman with short blond hair wearing a starched white shirt and black slacks. After she greeted them, she explained the two options for dinner.

They both ordered the caprese salad to start and the herb-roasted chicken breast as an entrée. Audra was happy for the poultry option because she didn't feel right eating fish in front of the fish. While she had the grilled vegetables, Damon opted for the mashed potatoes.

Throughout dinner, conversation flowed easily between them. At the end of the meal, Audra dabbed her lips and placed her napkin on the table. "That was delicious."

"It was," Damon agreed.

She studied him across the table. "Do I talk too much about my family?"

"Nah, you don't. It's nice. Sounds like you have a lot of fun."

"We do. I just don't want you to get bored."

"I'm not. I promise. Ready to walk off all this food?"

"I am. Should we wait for the server?" Audra looked around for the woman who had waited on them all night.

Damon stood. "No, we're good. Everything's taken care of. Come on."

Audra cradled the flowers in the crook of her arm and took Damon's hand. The same young man from earlier was waiting nearby, and he led the way through the halls. He explained about the animals they were seeing in the various exhibits and shared interesting facts, making the occasional joke along the way.

The last time Audra had been there, she had been preoccupied with keeping track of the children and making sure they all enjoyed themselves. This time, she felt like the kids must have felt. She oohed and aahed over the manta rays and stepped closer to the glass to examine the sharks and other sea creatures.

"This is amazing," she whispered. "I've been here before, but it's so different with no distractions and being able to leisurely walk through and check out the exhibits."

Damon nodded. "It's different for sure. I wish everybody could experience it like this."

"Me too."

The beluga whales were her favorite. They were playful, and one of them swam up to the glass, examining the couple in the same way they were examining him.

When he waved a flipper, Audra laughed. "Did you see that? He must know you're famous and wants an autograph."

Damon grinned. "Or he's trying to steal you away from me. Not gonna happen though." He slipped an arm around her shoulders and pulled her closer.

Audra wrapped her arm around his waist and nestled against his side. He was solid and warm, and she was completely at ease being close to him.

After the next round of explanations, the guide left them to explore on their own.

"How old is your daughter?" Damon asked as they strolled along.

"She'll turn six this summer."

He looked down at her with surprise.

"Yes, I had her young," Audra said. "I was nineteen. Having her put me on the straight and narrow path."

"You gave your parents hell, huh?"

"You could say that."

He tsked and shook his head. "It's always the quiet ones."

"I'm not bad... I don't know, I had a rebellious stage, I guess, and I stressed out my parents from time to time."

"It's a rite of passage for some people."

"Did you have a bad period?"

"Let's just say my parents were glad when I got really involved with baseball."

Audra chuckled softly to herself. "So, you don't have any kids?"

"Nope."

"Do you want kids?"

"One day. I can see myself as a dad."

Audra didn't know him well at that moment, but for some reason, she could see him as a father too. He was the strong, silent type, and she imagined he'd be the kind of father who didn't yell much, but with one stern word, his kids would straighten up. But there was a playfulness about him that would make him a fun dad, as well.

The evening ended too soon, and then they were on their way back to her house. The drive home passed quickly, and Audra longed for more time to talk and laugh with him.

At the doorway of her house, she clutched the flowers to her side and turned to face him while the driver waited. "I had a wonderful night."

"So did I." Damon stepped closer. "So next time I call or text, can I expect a quicker response?"

"Yes, Damon, if I see your text right away."

"Good."

Slowly, the smiles faded from their faces as they gazed into each other's eyes. Audra held her breath, her heart knocking against her ribs in a nervous rhythm.

Kiss me, she silently pleaded.

As if he heard her, Damon's eyes dropped to her lips, and without saying a word, he slowly bent his head and brushed his mouth against hers. In response to the fleeting touch, she inhaled deeply and curled her fingers into his shirt.

His hand slid under her hair to the back of her neck, and he pulled her against him. Audra parted her lips and invited him in, allowing his tongue to touch hers. God, she had been waiting for this—anticipating it the entire night from the moment he picked her up. She dipped her head back, savoring the deepening kiss, sliding one arm around to his broad back and pressing her aching nipples into his firm chest.

The need to be closer roared through her as their mouths devoured each other. One hand remained fastened around her neck while the other smoothed up and down her back and sent chills along her spine. His lips were hot and demanding, and when he gripped her ass cheek, a moan and violent shudder traveled through her.

Damon pressed her against the door and shoved his knee between her legs. Every inch of his hard length pressed into her lower belly, making her panties wet with want. She arched her hips and ground her core against him, silently pleading for more. Like a man staking his claim, Damon dragged a possessive hand over the swell of her breasts, and she gasped as desire thudded throughout her groin.

Suddenly, he lifted his head, and she released a soft whimper of disapproval. She wanted more. Her body ached with need, and between her thighs throbbed with hunger.

Damon looked down at her with dark eyes, his labored

breathing matching hers. "I better go now," he whispered huskily.

Audra bit her bottom lip. "Okay," she said, trying hard not to pout. What she really wanted was to sneak him upstairs and let him pound her through the mattress.

He dropped a quick kiss to her mouth, and she pressed her forehead against his. She couldn't remember ever feeling like this, or having this... *ache*, this *need*, to be close to a man. It was consuming her.

"Have a good night, beautiful." He whispered the words, his warm breath brushing her swollen lips.

Don't leave, she wanted to beg. Instead, she said, "You too."

He waited until she went inside before descending the stairs to the car. Audra watched through the window as the vehicle disappeared down the drive.

Touching her throbbing mouth, she relived the scrape of his beard on her skin and the intensity of the kiss.

Oh boy.

She was falling for him—completely and undeniably, without a shred of resistance.

Chapter Eleven

"How are things?" Claudia hung over the wall of Audra's cubicle, one eyebrow arched in inquiry.

Audra didn't have to ask what she meant. She knew right away that Claudia was inquiring about Damon. "Before I answer, how are things with you and Kent?"

Claudia blushed, looking very pleased with herself. "As you know, he's been very attentive ever since he thought he would lose me to a baseball player. That really shook him up, and our relationship has blossomed ever since. I can't complain. He bought me this." She extended a hand to show off a shimmering tennis bracelet.

"That's gorgeous. What was the occasion?" Audra asked.

"No occasion. He just wanted to surprise me."

"Look at you," Audra said.

Claudia giggled happily. "I can't stop smiling. I really took a risk because you know how much I love that man, but I couldn't continue with the way our relationship was going. He wasn't considerate of my feelings. Now our whole relationship has changed. I guess I had to let him know what I'd put up with and what I wouldn't, and that made him straighten up."

"I'm happy for you."

"Thank you," Claudia said with heartfelt appreciation. "Now, what's going on with you and Damon?"

"So far, so good." The past few weeks had been magical as they grew closer together.

"So he's nice and good to you?"

"Yes."

"No drama?"

"No drama," Audra confirmed.

Claudia lowered her voice. "Great in the sack?"

Audra paused. "We haven't..."

Claudia's eyes widened. "What? You've been seeing each other for almost two months now, right?"

Audra nodded. "We're taking things slow."

"Huh. No pressure, I guess."

"No pressure, but..." Audra sighed.

Initially, she had thought that going slow was a good idea because she hadn't been sure about Damon, but sexual frustration was now a constant companion. Every time she came into contact with him, her libido drove her to run her hands all over his delicious body. He reciprocated, driving her mad with teasing kisses and caresses. While her fingers trailed over the warm muscles beneath his shirt, his hands cupped her bottom and cradled her breasts. Every time they separated from each other, she was left wet, horny, and frustrated.

"I know. He's so hot," Claudia whispered.

Audra vigorously nodded, and they both erupted into giggles.

"Claudia, could you come here for a minute, please?" one of the managers called from his doorway.

"Sure thing." Facing Audra again, she rolled her eyes. "He

probably needs me to hold his hand while he makes a phone call."

Audra swatted her hand. "Stop it, you're so bad."

Claudia gave an evil laugh. "Yes, I am. Lunch later?"

"Yes."

"All right. See ya."

Audra watched her friend saunter toward the manager's office on the other side of the floor. She couldn't blame Claudia for being annoyed. He was one of the needy ones.

Gently gnawing on a fingernail, her mind wandered as she worked on the report for her supervisor. She rested her chin on her hand and looked at the last text exchange between her and Damon. She wanted more of him.

"Stop being greedy," she muttered to herself.

After all, each week they spent hours talking on the phone, especially when he was out of town. She had started going to his games, and when they were together, they made the best of every moment.

Dinner and dancing at an exclusive spot owned by one of his acquaintances, where they enjoyed themselves without the worry of someone taking photos or bothering him for an autograph. Then there was the private wine tasting at Chateau Elan, where they explored the winery's offerings and then had a delicious meal that evening. They also had a couple of double dates with his famous friends and their partners. Each and every time, he put forth significant effort to create a unique experience.

Audra fiddled with her pen. She needed to do the same. She needed to show how much he meant to her, and it was long overdue. She'd been busy basking in his attention and hadn't reciprocated the planning of their times together, partly because she was worried about doing too much.

That was her problem. She wished she were like her

younger sister, Monica, carefree and determined never to marry. But Audra imagined herself as a mom with several kids, being a domestic goddess—cooking and decorating. It wouldn't kill her to put forth a little more effort in the relationship. Stop taking and start giving.

Instead of working, she scoured the internet and came up with an idea. There was a retreat located thirty minutes south of Atlanta where she, Monica, and their mother had stayed before. Couples massages, farm-to-table cuisine, and quiet walks along the nature trails might be something Damon would enjoy. At lunch, she told Claudia about her idea, and she loved it.

By the time Audra arrived at home, she was excited about the trip for the next time Damon was free, but there was one more thing she wanted to do.

Her knowledge of baseball was practically nonexistent. Half the time, she didn't understand what was going on at the games, and there had been conversations when Damon talked to her about the sport, and she had no clue what he was talking about. She needed to rectify that.

Audra knocked on the bedroom door of her youngest sibling, Maxwell, and then pushed her way inside. "I need your help," she announced, standing in the middle of his room.

Unlike the typical teenager, her brother was a neat freak. His room was spotless—the bed made, his office supplies neatly lined up on the desk, all his clothes put away—and he knew when anyone had been in his room and moved an item.

The seventeen-year-old sat with his feet crossed atop his L-shaped corner desk and looked up from texting on his phone. His curls had grown long, coming down past his ears and falling across his forehead to touch his eyelashes.

"Ever heard of knocking first?"

"I did knock," Audra said.

"You're supposed to wait until I say you can come in," he said pointedly.

Audra moved closer. "If you don't want people coming into your room, lock the door."

"I'll be sure to do that. What do you want?"

"I need you to explain baseball to me."

His brow puckered in confusion. "Why? Since when are you into sports?"

"Do you know who Damon 'The Flash' Foster is?"

"Of course," Maxwell replied, sounding insulted. "He's one of the most popular players on the Atlanta Braves."

"He and I are dating, and—"

Maxwell dropped his feet to the floor and placed the phone on the desk. *"You're dating The Flash?* Since when? Did you know who he was when you met?"

"No, I didn't, but I do now. Anyway, we've been seeing each other for a couple of months, and he and I are getting close."

"Ew," Maxwell said with a wrinkled nose. "I don't want the details."

"I wasn't giving you the details, dork. Considering all the girls you mess with, you don't need to be judgmental."

He shrugged. "They say I'm charming."

"Anyway, as I said, I need your help. I want to understand the game, and I need a crash course. I've been reading up on baseball, but some of it I still don't understand, and I want to learn about Damon's stats and what's considered good and all that. Will you help me?"

Maxwell tapped his chin. "Hmm. You need my help."

Here we go. Audra blew out a sigh of resignation. "What do you want?"

A grin spread across his face. "A signed jersey from The Flash—one that he's actually worn."

Audra's mouth fell open. "Are you serious?"

"Yes. I need to smell his funky sweat all through the fabric."

"What the heck for?" Audra demanded.

"It's not for me! There's this girl—Sharonda—and she's a big fan of the Braves. She actually understands the sport," he said pointedly, which made Audra glare at him. "She goes to every home game with her dad. I've tried to talk to her, but she won't give me the time of day. If I give her a signed jersey from Damon Foster, maybe I'll have a shot with her. Help a brother out?"

Resting her hands on her hips, Audra said, "You're putting me in an awkward position."

"You scratch my back, I'll scratch yours. Or you can go back to reading Wikipedia or whatever you're using to study up on the game."

The silence stretched between them. Neither budged nor lowered their eyes.

"Deal." Audra extended her hand, and they shook. "When can we start the lessons?"

"As soon as I get the jersey."

"You're not gonna help me before?"

"Nope." Maxwell stood and walked toward his open door. "Get to work. You help me impress Sharonda, I'll help you impress Damon," he said, slipping out of the room.

Audra muttered curses under her breath. What was the point of having brothers when they were so difficult?

Shaking her head, she exited the room behind him.

Chapter Twelve

After the driver dropped Damon at his building, he took the elevator to his floor, anticipation thrumming in his blood. He couldn't wait to see Audra after being on the road for so long. He had called, told her what time his flight was landing, and that he'd love to see her. When she offered to wait at the condo, he quickly agreed and instructed the concierge to let her in.

He enjoyed their late-night talks, but he longed to hold and kiss her—which was becoming increasingly difficult because his body ached for more. His most vivid fantasy was of her riding him, her tousled mane of hair falling around her shoulders.

Truth be told, he hadn't gone this long without sex since high school. He wanted to make her toes curl and find out what his name sounded like when she screamed it in his bed. The only time she had been in his bed so far was one afternoon when she'd taken a nap there.

He pushed open the door and dropped his bag on the floor. "I'm home!"

Audra came flying around the corner with a bright smile

and leaped into his arms. Her legs wrapped around his waist as he cradled her bottom in his hands and kissed her hard and with passion.

"Damn, I've missed you," he muttered against her lips.

"I missed you too. Welcome home." She rubbed his bearded jaw and then slid her hand over his short-cropped hair. The comforting gesture immediately relaxed him.

"Thank you, baby." He sniffed the air. "What's that delicious smell?"

"Nothing fancy. A little something I threw together—pot roast, potatoes, and vegetables. I didn't know if you'd be hungry when you came home, but I figured you'd like a home-cooked meal."

Damon was speechless. Other than his mother and his personal chef, he couldn't recall any woman cooking a whole meal for him and was surprised she'd gone to all that trouble.

"Was it okay that I used your kitchen?" she asked.

Probably because he hadn't responded.

"Of course. Hell, I appreciate you doing that. Smells delicious."

Anxious to see her, he hadn't thought much about food because having someone waiting for him wasn't something he'd ever experienced before. Normally, he came home and warmed something from the freezer that his personal chef had prepared or stopped to pick up food from a local restaurant. Having her waiting for him made coming home sweeter.

Audra dropped to her feet and tucked a lock of hair behind her ear. "Put away your bag, change into something more comfortable, and I'll finish up in the kitchen. Then we can eat."

"Yes, ma'am." He kissed her neck, taking a deep whiff of her scented skin, and groaned.

She was driving him crazy. With her here, cooking a meal, and looking all sexy in tight jeans and a red top that hugged her curves, he was definitely appreciative. He wanted more of this kind of living.

He watched her walk into the kitchen and released a heavy breath. "Hang in there, bruh," he muttered, gently patting the front of his pants where his semi-hard penis threatened to embarrass him.

He took his bag into the bedroom and changed into sweats and a T-shirt. Checking his appearance, he smoothed a hand down his beard and then went to the kitchen. As he approached, he heard Audra talking.

"You *promised*, Kerry," she said, tension in her voice. She was standing in front of the range and holding the phone to her ear.

Her daughter's nickname was Keri, but Damon doubted that's who she was talking to. Probably her ex.

She heaved a sigh and dropped her head in defeat. As he hovered in the doorway, Damon immediately wanted to fix whatever was wrong.

"You don't get it, do you? She wants to see you. You're her *father*."

Her words confirmed what he had suspected.

Damon backed out of the kitchen to give Audra privacy, but he didn't like the sound of heavy disappointment in her voice. From the little he'd heard, he guessed that her child's father had flaked on plans, upsetting her—and not for the first time.

In the living room, he could hear her talking but could no longer discern the words. He stood in front of the glass doors looking out at the parking lot and waited until he no longer heard her voice. Then he returned to the kitchen.

"Hey."

"Hey." She pulled plates from the cabinet without facing him.

Damon walked over. "Everything okay?"

Audra nodded, but her hair had fallen across her cheek, hiding her expression from him.

Grasping her chin, he turned her head to face him. "Talk to me."

Her lower lip trembled, and she looked up at him with tear-filled eyes. "I was talking to my ex, Kerilyn's father. He promised to come see her next weekend, but now he says he can't because he has a gig out west. I didn't tell her that he was coming because I didn't want to get her hopes up until I was certain he'd follow through. I'm glad I didn't because *of course* he called to say he can't make the trip now. At least this time I didn't have to see the disappointment in her face and explain that it's not that her father doesn't love her or want to spend time with her, it's that he's so *busy*." Her face crumbled, and her voice cracked on the last word.

Damon pulled her into his arms. "I'm sorry, Audra."

"It's so unfair. She doesn't deserve this," she said, her voice trembling and thick with tears.

He held her for a few minutes until she was able to compose herself. Wiping her eyes, she looked gratefully at him. "I shouldn't be laying this on you."

"I don't mind, and I care about you. Because I care about you, I care about your daughter. I hate that she'll be disappointed. Some people become parents without understanding the magnitude of their decision and how the way they treat their child will affect them for years to come."

"They don't understand or they don't care," Audra said bitterly. She sniffed, and then a soft smile touched her face. "When she was a baby, I used to stand over her crib and watch her for hours."

"Hours?" Damon asked, teasing.

"Seemed like it. I couldn't get enough of watching her little fingers and toes and listening to her breathe. And you know how babies smell—oh, I loved her little baby smell. Every time I looked at her or held her, I was amazed by this tiny person I'd created. I still can't believe she's already six years old, has such a big personality, and is so loving. She loves kisses and hugs and is very affectionate." The light dimmed in her eyes. "I know she wants to give kisses and hugs to her daddy the way she gives them to me and her grandparents and her uncles, but he never makes time for her."

"Not everyone was meant to be a parent."

"True."

"It sounds like you have a great support system with your parents and your brothers. I know it's hard for her not to have her father in her life, but having a loving family—who shows her that she's loved—I promise you, it helps."

Audra looked at him with curiosity. "Are you speaking from experience?" she asked gently.

"I have two loving parents," Damon said, unwilling to divulge more. He brushed the tears from her cheeks with his thumbs. "The good news is, she isn't disappointed again like she's been in the past. She didn't know, like you mentioned."

"Yeah, I'm learning." She breathed through her lips and then fixed a smile on her face. "Ready for dinner?"

"I am, but are you sure you're okay?"

"Yes, and thank you for listening." She rose onto her toes and gave him a kiss.

Damon groaned and grabbed her bottom, pressing his lips against hers when she was about to pull away.

Audra licked his lips and placed her hands on his shoulders. "How about you fix our drinks while I prepare our plates?"

"All right." He slapped her bottom, and she yelped.

Chuckling, Damon went to the refrigerator. He poured

them each a glass of punch that his personal chef had whipped up and left for him.

During dinner, he told her about his trip, complained about where he thought he could have improved, and generally appreciated that she listened. After dinner, he washed the dishes and put away the leftovers while she relaxed on the sofa. When he joined her, she shifted closer and curled up next to him, resting her head on his shoulder.

He never would have thought a relaxing night at home would be enough to satisfy him, but with a full belly and his arm around Audra while they watched TV, he felt as if he'd won the jackpot. He pulled her closer. This was happiness. He had no interest in going out—not if she couldn't be there with him.

He hadn't seen himself getting married for at least a few more years, but there was something about Audra that made him look deep into the future and think about forever.

Forever with her.

* * *

"Baby, wake up."

Audra heard Damon's deep voice as if from far away. Her eyes fluttered open, and she lifted her head from his shoulder.

"Have I been asleep long?" Yawning, she covered her mouth and blinked rapidly. The room was dark because he had turned off the television. Beyond the windows, the lights of the city's buildings and moving cars brightened the night.

"Thirty minutes or so," Damon answered.

She knew why he'd woken her up. It was time for her to go.

His lips brushed over her forehead, slipped across her cheek, and moved lower to the corner of her mouth. She snuggled closer. She didn't want to go home. Leaving him was getting harder and harder, and tonight felt particularly difficult. She wanted to lose herself in his arms.

Everything leading up to this had been foreplay: the gifts he sent for weeks, the dinners, dancing, the weekend retreat, and the late-night phone conversations. He'd torn away her hesitations, and now she trusted him. Completely. And wanted to lose herself in his arms.

Audra stroked her hands down his chest. "Damon," she whispered.

"Hmm?"

Their eyes locked, and they both stilled. She didn't need to explain.

He immediately pressed his lips to hers, and she welcomed him with an open-mouthed kiss as her body became consumed with the heat of desire.

Chapter Thirteen

In the bedroom, Damon's hungry eyes ate her up as he peeled away her white bra and cobalt panties. She wished she had worn matching lingerie, but he clearly didn't mind.

He was disgustingly fine, his whole body covered in muscles and tattoos etched into his silky skin. And his package... Audra's eyes widened when her gaze swept the length of his thick thrusting shaft in the middle of his hips.

They tumbled onto the bed, but she pressed a hand to his chest to look into his eyes. "This is going to sound crazy, but I don't have a lot of experience. I've only been with Keri's father."

His eyebrows lifted in surprise, and then his expression changed from bewilderment to gentleness. "We don't have to rush. If you want to wait..."

"No, I want to," Audra said hastily. "I-I don't want you to be disappointed because I'm not like the women you're used to."

"You could never be a disappointment, and I'll teach you everything you need to know," Damon said with a smirk.

Lowering his head, he kissed her with passion and gently bit her lower lip. Then he soothed her by tugging the nipped flesh into his mouth. Pushing her legs apart, he ground his pelvis into hers, and she whispered her pleasure, clenching her fingers into his tattooed biceps and sliding the back of her foot along his hair-rough thighs.

She surrendered to him, arching her aching pelvis against his and pulling him hard against her so her breasts were crushed beneath the solid plane of his chest. The months of waiting and longing had worked her into a frenzy of need.

When his lips traveled down the length of her throat, she sighed and whispered, "I want you so much. Do whatever you want, Damon."

She meant every word. She needed him in a way she had never needed anyone else.

Damon feasted his eyes on her naked body, his thumb flicking across her full lips. He looked down at her with lust-drunk eyes. "You're so damn sexy—and so much more beautiful than I ever imagined," he said in a strained whisper.

He cupped her breast and stroked until the nipple hardened. He squeezed and fondled both breasts before latching his lips around her nipples and sucking until she sank her fingernails into his shoulders.

Peppering her skin with rough kisses, he used his tongue and teeth to tease and torture as he moved lower. He kneaded her curves, dragging his fingers over her heated skin until he reached between her thighs where she ached for him the most.

With his head bowed over her hips, he explored her wetness, using firm sweeps of his moist tongue. She gasped and writhed helplessly in the sheets, clamping down on his head as she scraped her fingers along his scalp.

Their lovemaking was sometimes gentle and sometimes rough as they explored each other's bodies with dizzying thoroughness. Audra slid over Damon, kissing his dark muscles, licking his skin, and smoothing her palms along his tattooed biceps. She kissed the sweep of his broad back and rubbed her mound against his firm ass like a cat in heat, marveling at his exquisite beauty and the masculine texture of his powerful physique.

Taking control again, he pushed her onto her back, and she let out an excited squeal.

"This right here," he said, grabbing a handful of her ass. "All this is gone be mine before the night's done. Every fucking last hole on this sexy body of yours."

She shivered with excitement and a little bit of dread but was determined to take whatever he dished out.

When he was sheathed in protection, excitement sparked in her blood, and she lifted her trembling thighs around his hips. She welcomed the crush of his body with open arms and parted her lips for another one of his demanding kisses.

The fingers of one hand fisted in her hair as she moaned, licking his earlobe and undulating her hips against his. Desire surged through her like a bursting dam.

"Now. I don't want to wait any longer," she panted.

He plunged into her, and her back bowed to meet him, taking him in as she lifted her body and allowed him to sink all the way to the hilt.

He commanded the pace, and she bucked beneath him, her arms clamped him, her teeth alternating between biting his strong neck and sinking into the muscles of his shoulder.

The scent of his skin was like heaven. The soft brush of his lips divine. But it wasn't enough. She wanted him closer. She wanted him deeper. So far inside her that she couldn't tell where she ended and he began.

From his groaning and panting, she knew he was with her all the way. They rocked back and forth on the soft mattress, the frenzied sounds of their lovemaking filling the room.

In one agonizing rush, a vicious orgasm ripped through Audra, and her body bucked uncontrollably as she clawed at him like a woman about to lose her mind.

Seconds later, she felt him swell inside her, and his release was equally as powerful. Their rough cries filled the room, his voice low and heavy with the sound of agonized pleasure spilling from his lips, his fingers digging into her fleshy buttocks as he ejaculated his release.

His arms collapsed, but he immediately rolled onto his back and dragged her on top of him. Audra relaxed, catching her breath and allowing her rapid heart rate to slowly return to normal.

* * *

Audra slipped from Damon's arms, and he looked at her through half-closed eyes.

"Are you leaving?" His voice was soft but deepened by sleep.

"I'm staying. I'm going to the bathroom," Audra whispered.

"Hurry back," he mumbled, fluffing the pillow before settling back down.

She smiled to herself. She could be a bit clingy, so it was nice to be needed and desired. His *Hurry back* confirmed he enjoyed cuddling and being close to her as much as she enjoyed cuddling and being close to him.

Audra took her phone into the bathroom to call her mother and let her know she wouldn't be coming home. She turned on the light and squinted against the sudden glare. Checking the mirror, she was startled to see her appearance—tousled hair, swollen lips, and sex-drunk eyes.

"You look a mess, girl," she whispered, giggling.

She was still amazed that this was the first time she and Damon had made love. They'd taken their time and gotten to know each other, and now... now she was on cloud nine and as giddy as a toddler with a fistful of candy.

That's what being with a good man did to you. *This* was happiness. *This* was a healthy relationship. She wasn't the only one making the effort. Damon was too.

She dialed and waited for her mother to pick up.

"Hello?"

"Hi, Mom. I... I won't be home tonight." She winced as she waited for the response.

"Okay." Rose drew the word out into two long syllables. "You're with Damon, I take it?"

"Yes."

Silence.

Leaning her back against the wall, Audra waited with a tight belly for the words that would dull her excitement. She hadn't exactly been a model daughter in the past. She'd had moments of rebellion and poor decision-making, including a run-in with the law once that had left her parents furious. To this day, she was surprised they didn't kill her.

They hadn't approved of Kerry, and when she ended up pregnant, their disappointment had been palpable. She knew, however, that they were the only people who came close to loving Kerilyn as much as she did.

"That's not a problem, I can watch her. She can keep me company while your father is out of town."

"Thanks, Mom."

"You're welcome, honey." Pause. "Be careful."

She added the warning in a lowered voice, as if she didn't really want to say it but couldn't stop herself.

Be careful.

Of what? Falling in love? Getting hurt? Making another mistake?

Audra wasn't worried. She'd had her doubts in the beginning, but Damon was right—he *was* different. Nothing like her ex.

"He's different, Mom. One day, I'll bring him over so you can meet him."

"We'd all love to meet him," her mother said.

"I'll plan for it one day, when he's not so busy. Can I speak to Keri for a sec?"

When Kerilyn came on the line, Audra explained to her daughter that she was going to stay out all night. Her daughter had a lot of questions, to which she explained that she was at a sleepover with a friend—the way Kerilyn sometimes had sleepovers with her cousins.

She blew her a kiss, and then Kerilyn returned the phone to Rose.

"Thanks for keeping her for me," Audra said.

"Not a problem. See you tomorrow."

Audra turned off the light and returned to the bedroom. She slipped under the covers, backed up to Damon, and pulled his arm across her waist.

She couldn't tell if he had woken up or not, but his arm tightened around her. They had taken a big step tonight. Soon —very soon—she would invite him to meet her family.

Chapter Fourteen

After checking the roast in the oven, Audra strolled into Damon's bedroom. He was sitting up against the headboard, and when she entered the room, a slow smile eased across his lips.

"You're wearing too many clothes," he said.

She looked down at the T-shirt she wore. It was one of his—blue with Nike in gold letters. "I'm naked under here."

"Like I said, too many clothes. You should be walking around this place completely naked."

"You're just horny all the time." She crawled across the bed and slipped under the covers, throwing an arm across his chest.

Damon pushed his hand under the T-shirt and rubbed her bare bottom.

Audra squirmed. "Behave," she said with a laugh.

"It's hard, baby. You're so damn fine." He squeezed her tight and kissed her forehead. "When's dinner gonna be ready?"

"I swear the only reason you keep me around is for sex and food."

"Mhmm. But when's that roast gonna be ready?"

Audra laughed again. "Thirty more minutes, greedy man."

His fingers traveled a light path down her hip. "You've spoiled me with all that good home cooking, woman."

"You have a personal chef."

"It's not the same," he said.

He'd told her that before, which always made her feel special.

"Well, you spoil me too." Audra kissed his cheek.

Earlier, they'd had a bout of intense lovemaking, and she was still in the hazy sex bubble that always enveloped her after she and Damon made love.

Made love.

That's how she'd started thinking about it lately. Not sex. Certainly not hooking up. They made love—whether it was slow or fast, rough or gentle, she savored every moment in Damon's arms.

In the past few weeks, they'd explored all kinds of positions, and most recently had incorporated the use of toys. With him, she was a willing pupil, and his lessons opened up a world she hadn't known existed.

Their relationship had also been discovered. A hazy photo of them had been taken inside a restaurant while they ate dinner. Probably a fan, though the image was shared by a popular gossip blog on Instagram. Audra wouldn't have known about it, but Damon shared the image with her after one of his exes—were they an ex if he claimed they were never in a relationship?—sent him the photo demanding to know who he was having dinner with.

According to the article, she was "the mystery woman with Flash Foster." Claudia thought the whole situation was exciting, but Audra was less enthusiastic.

Despite all that, she had no intention of cutting her time

with Damon. Finally in a healthy relationship, she was enjoying herself too much.

Damon tugged on his earlobe. "I'm thinking about getting another diamond, so I'll have one in each ear. What do you think?"

Audra lifted onto her elbow and took a good look at him. "I could see it."

"Yeah?"

"Two diamonds would be cute."

"Cute?" he repeated, sounding disgusted. "I'm trying to be sexy, not cute."

"*Fine*. You'll be sexy. You and your ego." She shook her head in mock annoyance.

"Thank you. Much better."

Audra played with a hair on his chest. "Hey, there's something I want to ask you."

"Shoot. You know you can ask me anything."

That wasn't entirely true. He tended to clam up whenever she tried to find out more about his childhood in Arkansas, which was odd, because he spoke fondly of his parents, and they seemed to have a good relationship. As a matter of fact, she had heard him talk to his parents on the phone a couple of times and couldn't detect anything less than warmth and affection in his voice.

She suspected something had happened to him as a child, but it was clear he wasn't ready to share with her yet. Meanwhile, she was an open book. She probably shared too much.

"I want you to come to dinner and meet my parents," Audra said.

She'd thought about it for a while and now felt confident enough in their relationship to introduce him to her family.

"Okay." He dragged out the word, a faint frown creasing his brow. "Are you sure?"

"Would you like to meet them?"

"Yes, but I want you to be sure about it. That means meeting your daughter, too, right?"

"Yes."

"So I finally get to meet the mini-Audra. Or that would be the mini mini-Audra. Get it, 'cause you're—"

"So short. Yes, I get it. Ha. Ha." He liked to tease her about her height.

He chuckled and then threaded his long fingers into her hair. The humor disappeared from his face, and his expression turned serious. "I would love to meet your parents and your daughter. Will you be doing the cooking?"

"No, and although you pay me lots of nice compliments, I'm not the best cook in my family. Don't forget I have a brother who's a chef."

"Bruno."

"Yes. He and I learned to cook from my mom. She cooks often, although we still have a chef and housekeeper. We have a whole staff, actually, though it's not as big as when I was growing up and everyone lived at home. Sometimes she cooks, and sometimes she uses the help. It depends on her mood."

"I don't care who's cooking. I just wanna eat. When were you thinking we should meet?"

"How about the next time you're off on Sunday, you can come over? That way, you can meet my brothers too. They can be a little overbearing, but I'll warn them ahead of time to be on their best behavior."

What she didn't tell him was that more than her brothers, she wanted her parents—especially her mother—to like him. Rose Santana's eyes spoke volumes, and Audra sensed the concern. She likely had done her research on Damon and worried Audra was making another mistake.

Sunday dinner would serve two purposes. Not only did

Audra want the man in her life to meet her family, but she also wanted to show them what she knew—that he was a funny, charming, kind soul, and she was lucky to have him in her life.

"I don't blame your brothers. If I had a sister, I'd probably be an asshole to any man she brought home."

"It doesn't help that my last serious relationship went up in flames." Audra grimaced.

He combed her hair with his fingers, smoothing the strands away from her face. "That's in the past. People make mistakes in relationships. It's part of life."

"Have you?"

He pondered the question. "I didn't make the mistakes. *Technically*, I was the mistake."

"Whoa, should I be worried?"

"Nah, you shouldn't be worried. I know we have something special. I'm not about to mess it up."

He always said the right things. Sometimes she worried he was too good at it. Too perfect. There had to be a flaw somewhere, but she hadn't found it yet. All she could do was wallow in the perfection of this relationship, a striking contrast to the mess that had been her relationship with Kerry.

She didn't have to hound Damon for attention the way she did when she and Kerry were a couple. Damon gave her attention freely, and she ate it up. She looked forward to his morning texts before he started training. "Good morning, sexy" or "Good morning, beautiful" always put her in a good mood for the rest of the day.

When they weren't together, they spent a lot of time on the phone talking—continuing to chat almost every day. In all this time, somehow, they hadn't run out of topics to discuss.

"You better not screw up," Audra said. She spoke lightly, in a teasing tone, but she was happier than she ever imagined and wanted this feeling to last.

"So your whole family will be at dinner, huh?"

"Not exactly. It depends on when you go. Ignacio is hardly ever around because he's an actor. Thiago—he works at my stepfather's company—is often out of the country, so he may or may not be there. Of course, you know Maxwell will be there."

"The one who wanted my jersey."

"Yes. He's planning on being a doctor. At least that's what he says. We'll see if he sticks to it. Then there's Ethan, the oldest. Monica might or might not be there because—well, she does her own thing. So, you up for it?"

"Yeah, I'm looking forward to meeting your family and Kerilyn. I've heard so much about them, I feel as if I know them already. I'm most excited to meet your daughter."

"Be careful, once she gets comfortable with you, she won't stop talking. You'll be begging her to stop."

"I doubt it."

He was staring up at the ceiling, and she studied his profile. The way he talked about Kerilyn prompted Audra to ask the next question.

"You said before that you want kids. How many?" she asked tentatively.

"Lots."

Her eyebrows shifted higher. "How many is lots?"

"At least five."

Interestingly enough, she wanted a big family too. "Your future wife is going to be busy," she teased.

He watched her for a moment, his dark eyes locked on hers. Then he smiled. "Yeah, she is."

Chapter Fifteen

"You don't need that," Audra insisted.

Damon silently disagreed, straightening his tie and critically studying his appearance. "You said your brothers are very protective, and I'm about to meet them, your parents, and your daughter. I want to make a good impression. I don't want them believing the stuff they read about me online, and I don't want them thinking I'm going to be like your ex."

He wore navy slacks and a white shirt, but a jacket and tie would be a nice addition.

Audra marched over, stood in front of him, and tugged off the tie. "You're going to be overdressed. It's Sunday dinner at my family's house, not the White House. I promise no one is going to judge you." She lifted onto her toes and kissed his stiff lips.

"You're sure?"

"I'm positive. You're usually such a confident person, it's cute that you're worried about making a good impression, but you have nothing to worry about. I couldn't resist you, and I know they won't be able to either."

"Don't try to butter me up," Damon grumbled. He looked at his reflection and then opened the top button of his shirt.

"You look great, hon. They're going to love you," Audra said.

He sighed. "All right, if you're sure, let's get out of here."

On the drive over, Audra told him that Ethan, Thiago, Bruno, and Maxwell would be at the house, in addition to her parents and Kerilyn. She warned that while her mother would be welcoming and kind, her stepfather was a toss-up because he could be protective like her brothers. Kerilyn was excited that she'd finally meet her mother's friend.

When they arrived at the property, Damon parked on the side of the house and followed Audra up the stairs and into the foyer. As soon as they entered, her parents approached.

"Hello and welcome. It's nice to meet you." Rose was a petite woman with a glowing smile.

"Nice to meet you, Mrs. Santana," Damon said, clasping her small hand in his.

"Please, call me Rose."

Benicio's greeting, while not cold, was cooler as he assessed Damon with curious eyes and a firm handshake.

He was a bearded Hispanic man with salt-and-pepper hair. "Nice to meet you," he said in accented English.

"Nice to meet you too," Damon replied.

"Please, come join us in the great room. We're waiting for the rest of the family." Rose extended a hand to guide them through a trio of arches toward the back.

The room contained a fireplace and seating arrangements that promoted conversation. They all sat down, with Audra and Damon on one sofa across from Rose and Benicio on the other.

He quietly took a deep breath, anticipating the questions that were coming.

"What's for dinner? The food smells delicious," Audra said.

On the way to the room, Damon had also smelled the meal, which reminded him that he hadn't eaten much because he had saved his appetite for dinner.

"Rodolfo prepared herb-crusted lamb chops with ratatouille, and for dessert, vanilla panna cotta with strawberry compote. Rodolfo is our chef," Rose explained to Damon.

Before they could continue the conversation, he saw movement out of the corner of his eye. Other members of the family strolled into the room.

"These are my brothers. That's Ethan, Bruno, and Thiago," Audra said.

Damon stood to greet them, and as he shook their hands, he remembered everything she had told him about her siblings. Ethan, the serious oldest brother, was quickly amassing a real estate empire. Bruno was a chef who looked like a younger version of his father with dark hair and gray eyes. Thiago worked with their father and was in town for a few weeks.

The sound of girlish giggles preceded the appearance of a little girl racing into the room with a teenage boy running behind her.

"Gotcha!" He scooped her up.

When he saw their company, he slowly lowered her to the floor.

"You must be Maxwell. I'm Damon." He extended a hand.

The teen grinned. "I know who you are. Nice to meet you. Did Audra tell you I said thanks for the jersey?"

"She did." Damon smiled at Audra's daughter, who looked up at him with curiosity as she sidled closer to her mother.

"Keri, this is my friend, Damon. Remember I told you about him?"

Kerilyn nodded and folded her hands in front of her. "Hello," she said in a polite voice.

"Hello, Kerilyn. It's nice to meet you."

Benicio came to his feet. "That's everyone. Now that we're all here, we can make our way to the dining room. I am starving."

They filed into the dining room, where a long table was set to accommodate them. Audra's parents sat at either end, and everyone else settled into chairs on each side of the table.

As Rose placed a napkin across her lap, she said, "I hope you brought your appetite, Damon. We have plenty of food."

"I do have a hearty appetite, ma'am, and I love a good home-cooked meal."

Staff entered and placed plates of watermelon and feta salad in front of each person.

Initially, the conversation centered around the absent family members. Ignacio was filming on location, and Monica was in Europe with friends, living her best life now that she had graduated.

Rose brought the conversation around to Damon. "Do you travel a lot during the season? I admit I don't know much about baseball."

Damon dabbed his mouth with a napkin. "We play 162 games, and half of those are away games."

"My goodness, you're gone quite a bit. He travels more than you, honey." She directed the comment at her husband.

Benicio grunted. "Now that you know the situation can be worse, maybe you will not give me such a hard time."

Rose pursed her lips. "All that traveling must be difficult," she said to Damon.

"It keeps me busy, that's for sure, but I make time for what's important." He shot a glance at Audra beside him, and she blushed as she placed a piece of watermelon in her mouth.

Rose's gaze bounced between them, but Damon couldn't read her expression.

"Do you have any children?" Bruno asked as a member of the staff lifted his empty plate from the table.

"No, I don't."

"Siblings?" Benicio asked.

"No. Just me, my mother, and father." He kept his voice neutral, but tension coursed through his muscles. He'd known they would ask personal questions, but he still became uneasy whenever those questions arose.

"But you date a lot of women," Thiago said slowly. He had a full beard and dark eyes, and more than once Damon had caught him staring, his gaze unwavering.

Audra's head snapped up, and an uncomfortable silence filled the room.

"I read about you online," Thiago said by way of explanation.

"I used to," Damon admitted.

He wanted to be careful how he spoke because he wanted to impress Audra's family, but he also wasn't about to let her brother intimidate him. This one, in particular, seemed to be an ass. At least the others were pretending to be nice.

"Used to?" Ethan, the eldest, latched on to the words. His eyes were cool and penetrating.

"Yes, past tense. Is there something wrong with dating?" Damon asked, laughing to lighten the mood.

"No, as long as all parties know what is going on and no one is playing games." Thiago again. What was the problem with this guy?

Damon met his gaze directly. "I don't play games off the field, and I wouldn't have come here to meet Audra's family if I didn't care about her."

Silence filled the room as both men stared at each other.

"Okay, that's enough," Benicio said in a warning tone, shooting a glance at his son. "Let's keep things civil. Damon is our guest."

Hopefully, that would be the end of the tension in the room. If Benicio hadn't interrupted, Damon had a sneaking suspicion the questions were about to become more antagonistic.

Audra squeezed his knee under the table. "Damon used to play for the Twins before he signed with the Braves."

He was impressed by how much she'd progressed in her baseball knowledge since they first met.

"Did you like it there?" Maxwell asked.

As he replied to the question, Damon relaxed. He told the family about his experience and how much he had appreciated signing with the Braves.

"My hope is to retire as a Brave," he said.

"I want to play baseball too." Kerilyn directed the statement to Damon. She sat between Ethan and Thiago.

"What position would you like to play?" he asked.

"I like to throw the ball," she answered.

"In that case, you'd like to be the pitcher."

She nodded vigorously. "I don't throw very far right now, but maybe I can throw far when I'm bigger."

Damon smiled across the table at her. "You can do anything you put your mind to. Size doesn't matter. Heart does."

A grin spread across her lips.

From then on, the conversation remained relaxed. The Connor-Santanas learned about Damon, and he learned about them, as well. He found out that Audra's Hispanic brothers had a connection to Colombia on their mother's side and learned about Ethan's dream of creating a multi-billion dollar residential development one day.

Maxwell's siblings teased him about the many girls he

dated, and Kerilyn added to the conversation by exclaiming that she was not looking forward to the end of summer vacation and going back to school.

When dinner ended, Damon said his goodbyes, and Audra walked him out. As soon as the door closed behind them, she flung her arms around his neck.

He hugged her back, laughing. "What's this for?"

She gazed up at him. "You were great. They love you."

"How do you know?"

"I know." She couldn't stop smiling. "Thank you for coming. I wanted them to see how great you are."

"I enjoyed myself, but things were a little rough at the beginning."

"That's just Thiago." Audra rolled her eyes. "He can be an ass, but if he's on your side, there's no one more loyal or who goes harder for you."

Damon nodded. "I can see that. He's got your back. Your whole family does."

"And Kerilyn likes you."

"She's a cutie. Maybe... if you're open to it, we could do something together with her one day."

She looked immensely pleased. "I would like that."

With one arm around her waist, Damon bent his head and kissed either side of her mouth. "I love being with you, Audra. Thank you for inviting me."

She pressed a hand to his jaw and kissed his lips, and he felt his body stir. She barely had to touch him for him to become aroused.

"I'll see you when you get back," she whispered.

He'd be on the road for the next five days and had never hated travel more than he did now because it meant being away from Audra. "See you then."

He gave her one more kiss and then jogged down the steps to his car.

Chapter Sixteen

Leaning back on her hands, Audra watched Kerilyn and Damon with the Princess Tiana kite he had bought.

He wore his cap backward and was dressed casually in a dark T-shirt and jeans for their afternoon excursion at the small park. Kerilyn was adorable in a shorts set, her mouth open wide in awe as she gazed up at the soaring kite.

He was so good with her. Patient. Friendly. Audra thought again about what a great father he would be.

"Mommy, look!" Kerilyn called out. Damon had let her take control.

"I see you."

Kerilyn pranced around the grass, looking back every so often at the kite overhead.

Minutes later, Damon jogged over and dropped onto the blanket beside Audra. "Hey, beautiful."

"Hey, handsome." She kissed his cheek.

He angled his chin toward Kerilyn. "I think Little Bit has the hang of it now."

"She has a good teacher."

"We didn't do so well with the baseball earlier, though." When they first arrived at the park, he'd shown her how to throw the ball and helped her catch it.

"I warned you she's not athletic," Audra said.

She watched Kerilyn stumble and then right herself. Her daughter glanced over at them.

"You're doing great, baby," Audra called out.

With the encouragement, her daughter started running again.

"I'm going to keep working with her on the pitching and catching," Damon said in a determined voice.

"That's up to you, but she's having a great time with the kite. Where did you find that particular one, anyway?"

"As soon as you told me that she liked Princess Tiana, I started my search. I found it at a specialty store and ordered it rush delivery so it would arrive by this weekend."

She vaguely remembered mentioning her daughter's preference when they talked on the phone. A man who listened. Unbelievable.

"I've never flown a kite before," Audra murmured.

"Never?"

She shook her head.

"I used to fly kites all the time. A few of the neighborhood kids and I used to make our own. One time, I made a Spiderman kite. Man, I was so proud of that thing. My boys and I would go to the park and fly our kites until it got dark."

"How old were you?" He so rarely shared stories about his childhood, Audra was anxious to learn more, especially hearing the excitement in his voice.

"About nine. The park was close to our apartment complex, so we walked over there and spent hours running around." He laughed, shaking his head.

Then she sensed a change in him. The smile slowly faded from his face, and his Adam's apple bobbed up and down as he swallowed.

"How long did you keep making kites?"

"Not long. I quit after a while."

"Why'd you quit? Sounds like you enjoyed it a lot."

"My Spiderman kite got messed up, so it wasn't fun anymore." He shrugged.

"How'd it get messed up?"

He tore at the grass. "Someone messed it up. He destroyed it."

"Oh no. Why? Who did that?"

"Nobody important."

"Was he a bully?" Audra asked, although she couldn't imagine anyone bullying Damon. But nine years old was a far cry from the twenty-seven-year-old athletic machine known as The Flash.

"No."

He didn't offer more information, and right then Kerilyn came running over. She dropped onto the blanket, panting.

"Did you see me?"

"Yes, we saw you. You did such a good job," Audra praised.

Damon took the kite spool from Kerilyn. "Very impressive. Good job."

He lifted his palm overhead, and Kerilyn gave him a high five.

Audra handed her daughter a small bottle of water to drink. As she gulped the liquid as if she'd been running through the desert for days, Audra watched Damon from the corner of her eye.

Why would someone destroy his kite? It was a very specific, mean thing to do. If they weren't a bully, who were they?

"Excuse me." A blonde woman and a little blond boy

approached. The woman looked embarrassed. "I'm sorry to bother you, but are you Damon Foster?"

"I am."

"See, Mommy? I told you!" the boy exclaimed.

"I hate to disturb you and your family, but do you mind if we have your autograph?"

"No, not at all."

"Thank you," the woman said with profound relief.

"What's your name?"

"Jason."

Damon scribbled a message and his signature on the notepad the woman handed him. "Would you like to take a picture?" he asked.

The woman looked like she was about to say no, but the boy perked up. "Yes!" he exclaimed.

Damon hopped to his feet, and the woman removed her phone from her purse.

"If you'd like to be in the picture, I can take the photo for you," Audra offered.

"Are you sure?" the woman asked.

"Yes. It's no problem."

Audra stood and took multiple photos of the three of them. She returned the phone to the boy's mother. "You have several to choose from."

"Thank you very much, and again, I'm so sorry to bother you."

"It's no bother. I appreciate the fans, especially the young ones," Damon said, fist-bumping the little boy.

After they left, Kerilyn looked curiously at him when he sat down again. "Are you famous?" she asked.

"A little bit," he replied.

"So that means you're very busy?" Kerilyn asked cautiously.

Sadly, Audra suspected she was thinking about her father, who was always too busy to spend time with her.

"Sometimes, but I like to have fun."

Kerilyn perked up. "Playing catch."

"Yes. And flying kites."

"And racing."

He arched an eyebrow. "Did you say racing?"

She nodded vigorously. "I run very fast. Don't I, Mommy?"

"She does. She's as fast as a cheetah," Audra confirmed.

Damon whistled. "That's fast. I don't know, though. I'm pretty fast myself."

"Not as fast as a cheetah," Kerilyn said. She hopped to her feet. "Bet you can't catch me."

"We'll see about that."

Kerilyn dashed off, her laughter echoing in the wind as Damon rose slowly to his feet.

"She's going to wear you out," Audra warned.

"I consider myself in peak condition, but I'm actually worried you might be right."

He jogged after Kerilyn, intentionally running slowly so she could stay ahead. Audra watched, laughing as her daughter zigzagged across the grass to escape him.

Finally, Damon picked up his pace and caught up to Kerilyn, sweeping her into his arms and spinning her around.

She squealed happily. "You got me!"

"I always catch cheetahs," he said.

He placed her back on the ground, and the two of them raced over to the blanket, with Kerilyn leading the way.

"Are you going to sit here all day?" Damon asked.

Kerilyn placed her hands on her hips. "Yeah, are you gonna sit here all day, Mommy?"

"Oh, so the two of you are ganging up on me?"

Giggling, Kerilyn grabbed Audra's hand and tugged. Groaning, Audra pushed to her feet.

"I want to race again," Kerilyn announced.

"How about from here to the picnic table this time?" Damon suggested.

"Count to three."

"Okay. One, two—" He broke off when Audra and Kerilyn sprinted away from him.

"Hey!" Damon yelled after them.

Laughing uncontrollably, Audra and Kerilyn bolted toward the table hand in hand.

They spent the rest of the afternoon flying the kite, tossing a ball, and chasing each other around the park.

Despite having a good time, Damon's story was never far from Audra's mind.

Who had destroyed his kite and why?

She wondered if she'd ever know the answer to that question.

* * *

Audra reached blindly for her ringing phone in the dark.

"Hello?"

"Hey." It was Damon.

Immediately, she smiled. "Hey. What time is it?"

"After twelve."

"Congratulations on the win tonight," she whispered. He was in Cincinnati, and they'd played the Reds.

"They almost whooped our asses."

"But you came back."

"We did. But that's not why I called. Why'd you send me that picture?"

"Did you like it?" she asked coyly.

"Hell, yeah."

She had texted him a photo of her looking over her shoulder in one of his T-shirts that barely covered her backside. She had never done anything like that before, but the teasing shot didn't involve any nudity, and Damon made her feel safe.

"Your butt looked amazing in my shirt, but you already know that."

She giggled softly. "You have a one-track mind."

"What was I supposed to think when you sent me a picture like that?"

"I was saying hello and showing you how well your shirt fit."

"Uh-huh. You're in trouble when I get back."

"Promises, promises."

She missed him so much, and hearing his deep, inviting voice made her long for him even more. The days between seeing him were too long, and the time they spent together was too short.

"You know, I was thinking about Kerilyn and came up with something else we could do together. How about you bring her to the game on Saturday? She can come down on the field and warm up with me and the rest of the team."

Audra heard the smile in his voice. She glanced at her daughter asleep in the bed beside her, arms spread wide and her chest rising up and down. Since the weekend they spent at the park, she had joined them two more times for activities in the past couple of weeks.

"She would love that."

"I thought so. I'll let her throw a couple of pitches and show off her skills."

Thanks to him, her daughter had gotten better at playing catch, and he was probably just as excited as Kerilyn would be. She couldn't be more pleased that he enjoyed spending time with her daughter, and Kerilyn enjoyed spending time with him too.

Audra laughed softly. "She's like her momma—not very athletic—so again, don't expect much."

"I won't be too hard on her." He sighed heavily. "Damn, I miss you."

"I miss you more," Audra whispered.

She wanted to say *I love you* but didn't want to be the first to spill what was in her heart—and did Damon feel the same? He would have to express that emotion before she mustered the nerve to tell him her feelings.

"What did you do today?" he asked.

Her answer led them into a conversation that lasted for two hours. When they finally hung up, Audra rolled onto her side. She couldn't adequately describe what she was feeling—maybe disbelief that this was her reality.

Thanks to Damon, she had learned to trust again. Trust her judgment. Trust in a man.

The clasp around her heart had loosened, and she was open to love. She was confident it was only a matter of time before he told her that he loved her.

She didn't want to get her hopes up, but she was fairly certain that he was the One. Their relationship was going so well, she couldn't imagine anything coming between them.

Chapter Seventeen

Audra's phone rang as she was placing her shopping bags in the back of her BMW. She had found some good deals, including a few trinkets that would make great gifts for friends.

She slammed the trunk closed and fished her phone out of her purse. Inwardly, she groaned when she saw her ex's name.

What does he want? she thought irritably.

"Hello?" she said as she climbed into her car.

"Hi, Audra."

"Can I help you with something?" She intended for the conversation to be short and kept her voice cool, the way she always did since she had given up hoping for a future where the two of them raised their daughter together.

"How are you?" Kerry asked.

Sitting in the parking lot, she stared out the window and frowned at the question. Since when did he care about her wellbeing? They rarely had much to say to each other that wasn't related to Kerilyn.

"I'm fine. How are you?"

"Doing great, actually. We kick off our European tour in a couple of weeks. Merch is selling well, and streams of our music are through the roof."

"Congratulations. Things are going well for you," Audra said.

Kerry was a great musician, and she wasn't surprised the band was seeing increased success. He wasn't only the drummer. He wrote some of the group's songs. She wished he worked half as hard at fatherhood as he did at music.

"If you want to speak to Keri, she's not with me. I'm out shopping. She's at home with Mom."

He cleared his throat. "Actually, I called to speak to you."

Now he really had her attention.

"Why?" Audra asked, suspicious.

"How are things with you and your baseball player boyfriend?"

He knew Damon's name but refused to say it. As a courtesy, she had told Kerry about Damon and Kerilyn meeting and the time they were all spending together. Not that she had much choice. Kerilyn talked non-stop about Damon, and Audra knew it was only a matter of time before she mentioned him during a conversation with her father.

"Everything with us is fine." *Not that it's any of your business*, Audra silently added. "Why?"

"I know you don't pay much attention to what's going on online, but er... I was doing a little research on your boyfriend—"

"Whatever you have to say, I don't want to hear it. I already know Damon was out there before we became involved. He's not like that anymore, so whatever dirt you think you've found, you can keep it to yourself."

"What I found isn't old, Audra. The two of you are in a relationship. An exclusive relationship, right?" her ex asked.

"Yes, Kerry." Audra was hard-pressed to keep the annoyance out of her voice.

"Are you sure about that?" He asked the question with quiet confidence.

A cold chill went through Audra, and she straightened in the seat. He sounded as if he had a piece of juicy gossip he couldn't wait to rub in her face.

She shouldn't entertain his messiness but heard herself ask, "What are you talking about?"

Kerry blew out a breath, as if what he had to say was difficult to divulge. "I don't know, Audra, it might be nothing, but... I saw a couple of photos of your man with someone else."

Her stomach tightened, and her heart started pounding. Still, she dismissed what he said. "You're making that up."

"I'm not. I wouldn't do that."

Audra swallowed hard, hesitant to ask the next question but knowing she had no choice. "What's in the photos?"

"Look, I didn't know if I should say anything since—"

"What did you see, Kerry?" Audra demanded, the pitch of her voice sounding particularly high inside the car.

He blew out another breath. "I saw a couple of photos of your man—with another woman. Looks like they were on a date, but like I said, it's probably nothing, Audra."

"It was one of those blogs, wasn't it? Which one?" she asked, her throat tight.

"It wasn't a blog. It was *People* magazine. I'll send the link, but don't overreact. Give the man a chance. Find out for sure what's going on before you go off on him. The photos could be innocent."

"Thank you for the relationship advice," Audra snipped. The gall of him.

"I know things didn't work out between us, but I don't want

to see you get hurt. I also don't want you to give up on a good relationship—assuming it's good."

"You're enjoying this, aren't you?"

"No, I'm not," Kerry insisted. "But I do find it interesting that you made all kinds of complaints about me and the pictures I took with other women. Then you end up with a man who obviously can't keep it in his pants. Before you, he was working his way through every Black model and actress in the country. I'm surprised he had time to play ball!"

"Are you done?" Audra asked through tight lips. She wanted this conversation to be finished and for him to send the link so she could see for herself these allegedly damning photos.

"Yes, I'm finished. I'll give my baby a call tomorrow when I have more time to talk to her."

"I won't mention it in case your plans change."

He muttered a curse. "You couldn't help yourself, could you? Guess what, Audra, if I didn't work so hard, I wouldn't be able to send those monthly child support checks. So maybe act a little more grateful that I'm not one of these men out here refusing to take care of his kid."

His words bristled with anger, which kept Audra quiet. No point in arguing with him anyway because her head was spinning, preoccupied with chaotic thoughts about his Damon accusation.

Please let it be innocent. Please let it be innocent.

She desperately hoped Kerry was just being messy. Even if the photos looked bad, there was probably a very reasonable explanation.

"I can see you don't want to talk to me anymore. I'll hang up and send the link," Kerry continued.

"Thank you." *Hurry!*

Audra stayed in the parking lot, unable to drive away until she received the text. When it came through five minutes later, she hastily clicked the link and read the headline: "It's a Home Run! Flash Foster and Supermodel Nami Deagan Heat Up NYC Party!"

Audra scrolled lower to the photo of Damon, who looked sexy as hell—but when did he not?—in a light-colored shirt open almost to his waist, exposing several gold chains against his chocolate skin.

With him was a woman she didn't recognize, but the caption identified her as Victoria's Secret model Nami Deagan. She was as tall as Damon in a pair of high heels, the two of them dancing up close, Damon's arm resting on her waist. Nami wore a champagne-colored dress with spaghetti straps that shimmered against her umber skin. The short dress stopped mid-thigh and showed off her long legs. There was plenty of room around them, as if the other partygoers had cleared out of the way to give them space to dance.

Another photo showed the couple hand in hand, leaving the venue, with Damon leading the way. The wind blew Nami's straight raven hair as they hustled out the door. Knowing Damon the way she did, he was probably horny from grinding on Nami while they danced, so he was taking her to a place where he could satisfy his sexual appetite.

Tears blurred her vision.

They looked amazing together—two impossibly beautiful people basking in the glow of flashing cameras. Audra desperately wanted to believe the photos were harmless and that there was nothing more to the story, but betrayal and disappointment settled in her chest like immovable twin boulders, squeezing the air from her lungs. A hollow ache spread through her. Seeing Damon with the supermodel suggested that she had been wrong about him—about them.

She didn't bother to read the article. She didn't have to.

What more evidence did she need to see that he couldn't be trusted—which she should have known?

The allure of multiple women and living on the edge was too seductive. She had learned that lesson with Kerilyn's father but had wanted to believe in the fairytale. Damon had convinced her he was different.

When was she going to learn her lesson? How many more mistakes did she need to make before she understood that men —especially those focused on their careers and courting the limelight with all that entailed—could not be trusted?

And she'd introduced him to her family. He'd met her daughter.

She groaned, slumping in the seat.

"Dammit, Audra, you're such an idiot," she muttered, blinking back tears of anger and hurt.

What a fool she had been to believe this time was different. What a fool she had been... to fall deeply and madly in love with him.

Chapter Eighteen

hit. Shit. Shit.

In the locker room after taking his shower, Damon stood with a towel wrapped around his waist, staring at the screen of his phone and the text that had come in from Audra. She couldn't have been clearer, though she hadn't typed a word. All she had done was send the link to the *People* article.

Why had they posted it so soon? The photos weren't supposed to go to press until next week's issue. Instead, they had published them online right away.

"Yo, Flash, you coming out with us tonight?" Eddie asked from the doorway.

Damon lifted his attention from the screen. "Nah, I got something I need to take care of."

"All right, *hermano*. If you change your mind, you know where we'll be."

Damon finished getting dressed and grabbed his bag. On the way to the car, he called Audra, but the phone rang and went to voicemail. He called two more times on the way to the hotel. Each time, no response.

Head throbbing, he entered his room and tossed his bag on the floor. He paced the carpet in frustration, trying to figure out what to do. They had two more games against the Mets, and then they were headed to Ohio to play the Guardians. He wouldn't be back in Atlanta for another week.

He yelled out a curse and lifted his hand above his head to toss the phone across the room. At the last moment, he thought better of it and lowered his arm.

Maybe she was busy. He'd wait a while before calling her again.

Damon ordered room service and ate dinner while reviewing film to prepare for tomorrow's game. Every so often, his eyes strayed from the iPad screen to the phone on the table, as if he'd miss a text or call from Audra with the device right next to him.

When he finished eating, he placed his dishes outside the door and called her again. She picked up this time, and the relief that flooded his veins forced him to drop onto the bed.

"Audra, baby, I know what you're thinking."

"You don't know what I'm thinking."

He was accustomed to her excitement every time he called, so the lifeless, dull sound of her voice gutted him.

"You have to let me explain," he said.

"What is there to explain? The photos are self-explanatory. You and Nami looked cozy dancing at the party, and you were holding her hand as you left. Probably to go somewhere to screw her brains out, am I right?"

"No," Damon said immediately. "You're wrong. Listen to me, remember when I told you that sometimes as celebrities we create our own publicity? This is one of those situations. The whole evening was a stunt arranged by Nami's people."

"Why would Nami's people arrange something like that?"

At least she was willing to listen, so Damon gladly

continued explaining. "Nami signed with a new designer. They're small and have a limited budget. We spent ten minutes at the venue and then left, but being seen there was great publicity for them because the dress she was wearing was one of their designs."

"You mean the slip?" Audra asked.

Damon winced. Admittedly, the dress had been short and showed off the model's slender frame. "It's a dress. A one-of-a-kind," he murmured.

"Good for her for finding a creative way to publicize the outfit, but why did you participate in something like that if you're in a relationship?" Audra demanded.

"Hardly anyone knows about you and me, Audra, so I didn't see the harm in helping her out."

"Oh, is that what you call *helping her out?* You took her dancing?" she asked with a sarcastic edge to her voice.

Damon temporarily closed his eyes. This was going to be hard as hell. With other women he'd dated before, he could tell them anything—the truth or lies, didn't matter—and they always understood. They always forgave him. It was clear he would not have such an easy time with Audra.

"You know what I mean," he said.

"And you don't get anything out of this arrangement? You did it because you're a nice guy?" Audra asked.

"I do get something out of it, but not what you think. I've been figuring out ways to generate income after baseball. I've done a little modeling, but I want the opportunity to do more. My agent and Nami's manager are old friends. Nami's manager agreed to help me make those connections in exchange for getting eyes on Nami while she was in New York."

"You must be really excited to start modeling because you looked like you were having the time of your life. The way you two were smiling at each other—if that was fake, you deserve Academy Awards."

"Audra, of course I was acting."

Silence reigned on the other end of the line. He waited her out.

"You should have told me," she said.

"I didn't have time. It all happened so fast. My agent tossed me the idea, I said yes, and Nami and I went out after the game. The photos weren't supposed to be printed until next week, so I thought I'd have time to explain everything to you."

"Well, you didn't have time, and maybe the whole world doesn't know about our relationship, but my family does. Do you have any idea how humiliated I'll be if any of them see those pictures? And you know what, if you're such a great actor, how do I know you're not acting when you're with me?"

Elbows to knees, Damon buried his face in one hand. "You know me, baby. *Come on.* I would never hurt you like this. I would never risk *us* and what we have." He blew out a breath. "How did you find out about the photos anyway?"

"Kerry called and told me."

Her ex. *Motherfu—*

"I'm glad he did because I might not have seen them otherwise. To be honest, Damon, I don't know if I can trust you."

His head snapped up. "What are you saying? Are you going to let this ruin our relationship? Audra, I don't want our relationship to end over a damn misunderstanding."

"It's more than a misunderstanding! You were with another woman under very suspicious circumstances. I don't travel with you, so how do I know what you're doing when you're at the away games? You're gone for days at a time."

"Baby—"

"I have to figure out if what you're saying is true, and I'm

not so sure." The finality in her voice propelled Damon to his feet.

"Listen to me. I screwed up. I admit it. I take full responsibility. I should have called or texted you right away. That's my bad, but I'm not willing to give up on us. Tell me what to do." Damon held his breath as he awaited her reply.

"I'm not sure what you can do. Maybe nothing." Her voice trembled.

"Don't say that, sweetheart." His world was crumbling around him, and there was nothing he could do? This couldn't be happening!

"I have to go," Audra said in a thick voice. She sounded on the verge of tears.

"Audra, baby—"

"Good night, Damon. I need time to think. Don't call me for a while."

"Don't say that. Baby—"

Click.

The line went dead. The sound was like a kick to the heart.

He remained frozen with the phone to his ear, unable to move. The silence on the line was deafening, each second dragging by in a never-ending loop as realization cut through him like a knife.

I'm going to lose her.

He lowered his hand. Numb.

He should have told her right away. Even if *People* magazine had printed the photos next week as originally planned, someone at the party could have shared pictures of him and Nami online beforehand, which could have also gotten back to Audra.

He hadn't been thinking. Over the years, he'd grown accustomed to living his own life and doing his own thing without answering to anyone. Being in a monogamous relationship was... different. Life didn't center around Damon "The Flash" anymore. Every major move he made affected not only him, but *them* as a couple.

Mind racing, he ran a hand over his short-cropped hair.

A misunderstanding couldn't, and wouldn't, be the end of them. He refused to let their relationship end like this. He had to convince Audra of the truth, that's all.

He'd reach out to her when he returned to Atlanta and force her to talk to him face to face.

Chapter Nineteen

Audra finished combing Kerilyn's hair into long twists and snapped a clip at the end of the last one. Her daughter was excited that she would be spending time with her cousins on their farm. She loved feeding the chickens, milking the cows, and chasing the goats around the yard. For her, the experience was an adventure—something different from the norm. For them, managing the farm was work, which had expanded beyond their roadside stand selling fruits and vegetables.

In recent years, they had added a petting zoo, the option for guided tours, and a small store that sold baked goods made from their yield. In the fall, they offered wagon rides throughout the property and allowed people to pick their own apples for a fee.

Kerilyn hopped up from the ottoman and took a look in the hand mirror.

"I look pretty," she announced with a smile.

"Yes, you do. Always," Audra said. "Time to get dressed. Cousin Joe will be here soon to pick you up."

Kerilyn scampered away and raced up the stairs ahead of

Audra. In her pink-decorated room, Audra added a few more items to her daughter's small suitcase before zipping it shut.

"That's everything?" she asked Kerilyn.

Her daughter nodded.

"You're sure? You won't be coming back before the weekend is over."

"I'm sure."

"You're not taking any stuffed animals this time?"

Kerilyn shook her head. "I don't need them."

The doorbell rang.

"That's Cousin Joe. Let's go," Audra said.

At the top of the stairs, they saw Cousin Joe—a couple of years younger than Audra—being welcomed inside by a member of the household staff. Joe worked on the farm with his parents and younger siblings and was dressed in overalls and a baseball cap, looking every bit like a country boy.

"Hey, Joe," Audra called as she carried the suitcase down the stairs.

"Cousin Joe!" Kerilyn raced over and gave him a big hug.

He embraced her and patted her back. "Hi, Keri. I hope you're ready, because we have a lot of work to do," he warned in his slow drawl.

"I'm ready!" Kerilyn straightened up like a soldier, indicating she could handle whatever he tossed her way.

"She's been talking about this weekend ever since you called," Audra told him.

Her mother walked into the foyer carrying a paper sack with a handle, a local boutique's name emblazoned on the front.

"Hi, Aunt Rose," Joe said.

"Hi, Joe. How are you?"

"Getting by. This heat ain't no joke."

"You're not working too hard, I hope," Rose said with sympathy.

He laughed easily and placed a hand on Kerilyn's shoulder. "Nope. I leave that for the younger ones."

That wasn't entirely true, but Joe was the kind of person who didn't like to toot his own horn. He was the main reason the family had expanded beyond the stand and now included other ways to make money from the farm. He had suggested adding strawberry picking for next year, which would be another stream of income for the family.

Rose handed over the bag. "This is for your mother. It's that new hand cream she wanted."

He took the package. "I almost forgot she told me to make sure I brought it back." Grasping the handle of the suitcase, he gazed down at Kerilyn. "Ready to go?"

She nodded, and Audra and her mother watched from the doorway as they descended the stairs and climbed into Joe's truck. As they drove away, Kerilyn waved, her smile as wide as her entire face.

Rose shut the door. "She gets so excited about these trips, doesn't she?"

"She loves the idea of working on the farm. If she had to do it for real, I doubt she'd have the same enthusiasm. Joe said they might have her help at the roadside stand this time—handing over purchases and taking money—that kind of thing."

"She'll learn a lot, that's for sure."

"I think she's more excited about seeing her cousins and running around the property," Audra added.

"You kids were like that when you were little too. You loved being on the farm."

"I remember."

Rose's eyes narrowed. "Everything okay?"

Her mother was very perceptive, but Audra tried none-theless to hide her feelings. "Yes. Why do you ask?"

"You seem rather quiet lately, and you didn't go to work yesterday. You're not sick, are you?"

She had skipped work, unable to deal with all of her emotions and knowing she needed to make a decision about her and Damon before he returned to Atlanta.

"I'm fine. I..." Audra's voice faltered. The concern in her mother's voice and face was too much. Why fight it? She needed someone to talk to. Her shoulders drooped lower. "Can we talk?"

"Of course."

Rose ushered her through the arches that led to the rear of the house. Leading the way into the great room, she sat on the sofa, and Audra settled beside her.

"What's wrong?" Rose asked, her voice gentle.

"Promise not to say I told you so?" Audra asked with a self-deprecating laugh.

"Never," Rose said.

Audra pulled air into her lungs and launched into the story about Kerry sending her the photos of Damon and Nami.

When she finished, Rose said, "That's why you've been so quiet."

"Yes," Audra admitted. "I should have known better," she said in a sullen tone.

"Has Damon tried to explain at all?" Rose asked.

"Yes, but I'm not sure I believe him." She told her mother about their phone conversation.

Since then, Damon had reached out a couple of times, but she ignored his texts. She had meant it when she said she wanted time to think without him influencing her decision-making.

"I know he swears the situation with Nami was nothing

more than a publicity stunt, but how many times did Kerry tell me some groupie was his friend or that I was misreading a photo of him in an intimate embrace with a 'fan'? I don't want to deal with those feelings anymore. He turned me into someone I didn't like—angry, bitter, *hurt*. This situation with Damon has me headed in the same direction." She swallowed and shook her head. "I-I really liked him, Mom."

Rose's eyes were sympathetic. "You more than liked him, didn't you?"

Biting her bottom lip, Audra nodded.

Rose stroked her hair. "I know. I could tell."

"I can't avoid him forever, but he won't be back for a couple more days. That gives me time to figure out what I want to do."

"What happens when he comes back?" Rose asked.

"I don't know," Audra said, head bent as she picked at her thumbnail. "I have to talk to him at some point. I'll... wait until I absolutely have to, I guess. Or maybe he'll give up."

Rose covered Audra's hands and gazed into her eyes. "Say the word, and your father will make sure he doesn't come anywhere near you if that's not what you want."

Benicio would probably hire a bodyguard or take some other drastic measure to keep him away.

"I know. I'll let him know if I need help," Audra whispered, grateful that she had support if she needed it. "How could I have been so wrong again?" She didn't really expect an answer but hoped her mother would have advice to help her feel better.

Rose squeezed her hand. "Love is always a risk, no matter who you fall for. Taking a chance on love takes courage, and you're not wrong to open your heart to someone."

A tear rolled down Audra's cheek, and she angrily swept it away. "But my relationships keep ending in heartbreak. Maybe

I'm not meant to be with someone else." Her shoulders slumped.

Looking deeply into her eyes, Rose squeezed her hands again. "Don't you *dare* believe that. There's much more in store for you than this moment of pain. Sometimes the wrong person has to come along to make you aware of what you truly deserve, and then you find the right one, and poof! Everything makes sense." She smiled gently. "It's okay to grieve and cry and get it all out, but don't lose faith in yourself or in love. When the right man comes along, he'll show you through his actions, not just his words—how important you are to him and how much he loves you and wants to be with you."

"Thanks, Mom."

Later, lying in bed and staring up at the ceiling, Audra made a decision. It was time to move on from Damon, but the two of them needed to talk.

When they did, she would let him know how much he had disappointed her, and then she'd walk away.

To be free for the right man to come into her life.

Chapter Twenty

The following week, Audra walked out of the building with her co-workers. To keep her mind off Damon, who she hadn't heard from in several days, she agreed to go out for drinks with Claudia and Kyrie, one of the guys from the mailroom.

However, Claudia received a call from Kent. He had popped in for a couple of days to surprise her. Her friend didn't have to say a word. Both Kyrie and Audra waved her off to go be with her man, laughing as she practically ran across the street to collect her car and go home.

"He better marry her," Kyrie said.

"Agreed. Because boy, does she love that man."

"Did you still want to go grab drinks? You can cancel if you want," Kyrie said.

"Are you trying to get rid of me?" Audra asked, narrowing her eyes with playful suspicion.

"No way. I've been looking forward to this all afternoon."

"Same. A couple of hours tossing back drinks and eating fatty food that's no good for me is exactly what I need."

"Same. Today was rough, wasn't it?"

"It sure was."

All the execs were in a bad mood as they worked on a multi-million dollar deal. Negotiations with their partner in Argentina were tense, and an agreement seemed on the verge of falling apart. Audra didn't know much about the details because she wasn't privy to them, but she'd overheard Benicio and Thiago talking about the issues, and they both planned to fly down to South America to smooth the negotiations if they couldn't come to an agreement within a few days.

She and Kyrie walked a couple of blocks to a small tapas place nearby. When they entered the restaurant, the hostess seated them right away, and they ordered drinks.

Kyrie sighed as he sipped his frozen margarita. "Damn, I needed this," he said.

Audra indulged in a huge sip of her chocolate martini and sighed too. "So good," she whispered.

As she replaced the drink on the table, her eyes landed on a sight she never expected: Damon, walking toward them.

Her breath caught, and her heart knocked against her chest as she drank him in, eyes absorbing every inch of his tall, athletic frame in a long-sleeved white shirt and charcoal pants.

He stopped beside their table and locked eyes with her. "Hi," he said.

"Hi." She swallowed and shot a look across the table at Kyrie, who appeared confused.

"We need to talk," Damon said.

"Right now isn't a good—"

Slamming a hand on the table, Damon leaned toward her, giving his back to her co-worker. "Don't play games with me, Audra. You haven't responded to my last two texts, and I know you got them."

"Now is not a good time, Damon."

"Well, since I can't reach you to set up another time, right now will have to do."

"Hey, what's your problem?" Kyrie asked.

Hand still resting on the table, Damon shot a glare at him over his shoulder. "I don't have a problem. Do you?"

Kyrie's frown deepened. "Do I know you?"

"No, you don't." Damon returned his attention to Audra. "Can we go somewhere and talk?"

"I already ordered—"

He leaned closer. "Or do I have to haul you out of here?"

By the look in his eyes, she didn't doubt he meant the threat, and the last thing she wanted was to make a spectacle of herself. Several customers nearby were already turning around and whispering, having recognized him.

"Fine, I'll come with you." She tossed an apologetic look across the table to Kyrie. "I'm sorry, I need to go. When my food comes..."

She rummaged in her bag for her purse, but before she could pull out any cash, Damon dropped two bills on the table. "That should cover whatever she ordered and your food too."

Then he took her arm and pulled her none too gently from the chair.

"Excuse you," Audra muttered out the side of her mouth as they walked briskly toward the front door, her shorter legs barely keeping up with his.

He didn't say a word. He kept walking and didn't release her until he'd exited the building and marched her in front of the window of a closed store next door that sold trinkets and home furnishings.

Audra rubbed her arm. "You didn't have to grip my arm so hard."

"You're fine," Damon said dismissively, which infuriated her.

"You behaved like a caveman. I'm not fine."

He flicked his gaze over her appearance. She was wearing her hair straight and sleek today, one side tucked behind her left ear. She had kept her makeup to a minimum but added a hint of color to her lips. Her outfit was simple but molded to her figure—plaid pants and a bright-colored top.

"You look beautiful. You're fine," he remarked.

Her face heated up, and she mumbled a "thank you," then mentally kicked herself. She didn't need to thank him for anything. She was mad at him.

"What do you want?" she asked.

"To talk. To explain about Nami."

"What is there to explain? You were on a date with a Victoria's Secret model, weren't you?"

He looked frustrated. "I already explained we weren't on a real date."

"Right. I forgot." Audra crossed her arms over her chest.

"Nothing is going on between me and Nami. Nothing happened that night. Do you forgive me?"

His voice was antagonistic, as if she'd done something wrong.

Two couples came toward them. When they had passed, Damon lowered his voice. "I didn't cheat on you."

"That's the thing, Damon. I don't know if you did or not. You say that night was all orchestrated for publicity, but how do I know that?"

"Because I'm telling you. You have to trust me."

"No, I don't have to trust you. That's where you're wrong. Trust has to be earned, and—"

"What have I done that suggests you can't trust me?"

"Are you serious? Let's forget about the fact that you didn't do commitment and were technically a mistake for other women—your words, not mine. Every time I try to have a deep conversation with you about your past or your family, you clam up! So no, I don't completely trust you because you act like you're hiding some deep, dark secret. For all I know, you could be involved in criminal activities."

Shaking his head, he bit his lip as if biting back words of anger. "You don't really believe that."

"No, I don't, but that doesn't change the fact that you keep parts of yourself from me."

"So because I don't tell you my deepest, darkest secrets, you think I'm lying about Nami?"

"I've been here before. I told you about my ex, remember? Kerilyn's father."

"I'm not him!"

"That doesn't mean I don't see the signs and recognize similar behavior. The problems start like this, with a perfectly reasonable explanation that makes it seem as if *I'm* overreacting, but the truth is, I'm not. If you cared about me—about us—you would have told me about the deal with Nami ahead of time."

"I told you that I couldn't. I can't tell you about every single move I make before I make it."

"We talk almost every day!" Audra screamed, frustrated.

"Time." Damon slammed the back of his right hand into his left palm. "I didn't have time to tell you before she and I went out."

"Time." Audra slammed the back of her right hand into her left palm. "You should have made the time to tell me. A text would have been enough!"

He looked like he wanted to throttle her, but she stared him down, unintimidated.

"I told you from the beginning there's a lot of bullshit I have to put up with from the media—innuendo, lies, gossip."

"And you used it to your advantage in New York. But

here's the thing, Damon, you say you want to be in my life, but do you really? You can't continue doing things like that. I will *not* be embarrassed on a national stage."

"That's what this is about? You're embarrassed?"

She shook her head in disgust. "No. It's about trust, and I cannot trust you right now. You keep things from me, but more than that, before you and I started seeing each other, there were already so many women in your life. I was a fool to think you would settle down and want to be with one woman. You're young and having the time of your life."

"I have the time of my life when I'm with you. Why can't you see that?"

"I'm convenient."

"That's not true," he grated.

"Why deny it? Enjoy your freedom and your ability to attract women. You're young and rich, and you should enjoy yourself. But I want more."

She hadn't realized how important it was to her until she said the words out loud, and her heart seemed to swell in her chest—the pain of knowing they weren't on the same page tearing through her. She did want more. She deserved it.

She deserved the husband and the kids and all the things she wanted. She recalled her mother's words. *There's much more in store for you than this moment of pain.*

"I don't want to see you again."

He stared at her in shock. "You're kidding me, right?"

Sometimes the wrong person has to come along to make you aware of what you truly deserve...

That didn't only apply to her. It applied to him too.

"I mean it. Go live the life you want, and eventually, you'll find your person. We both will."

She tried to walk past him, but he grabbed her arm.

"I don't want anyone else."

Audra yanked her arm away. "Stop!" He seemed surprised by her anger.

She had never given Kerry the verbal thrashing he deserved, mainly because he was Kerilyn's father, and she wanted to maintain a good relationship with him so her daughter would have him in her life. So, a small part of her needed this outlet—needed to let off steam and yell and give Damon a piece of her mind.

Resting a hand on her hip, she glared at him and jabbed her finger at his face. "I will not, I mean absolutely *not* turn a blind eye to your indiscretions. You want to hoe around while in a committed relationship, look elsewhere. I am *not* the one."

"So that's it. We're done? You're going to walk away from us—after months of being together. Okay, Audra, cool, but you're making up excuses, and you know it."

"I am not making up excuses. I told you—"

"Yeah, yeah, I know you have trust issues. You think you're the only person in this relationship with trust issues? You think you're the only one who's ever had people you care about hurt you? You know what, fuck you, Audra."

Her mouth fell open. "Fuck you, Damon. And go to hell!"

"No, you go to hell."

They glared at each other, chests heaving, their angry curses hanging in the air between them.

Then the gravity of the situation hit her. They were through. Done. Kaput.

"Don't ever call me again," Audra said in a choked voice.

The angry mask slipped from his face for a fraction of a second, and he swallowed hard before the mask slipped back into place.

"I won't."

Audra spun on her heel and rushed away as fast as she could so he wouldn't see her burst into tears.

Chapter Twenty-One

"Fuck her. Excuse me, Pops." Agitated, Damon paced the length of his living room with the phone glued to his ear.

His father had brought up Audra, and the curse word slipped out. He was accustomed to using colorful language around his father, but he'd never dropped the F-bomb before.

Chadwick let out a sympathetic sigh. "Are you telling me you're done with Audra?"

"It's been four weeks since I saw her. My calls go to voicemail, and she doesn't respond to my texts. I'm fairly certain she blocked me."

Despite the blunt way they had spoken to each other, he had reached out with the hope of reconciliation. He figured that since he had cooled off, she probably had too. Clearly not.

"I'm done chasing her. I told her the truth, and she doesn't believe me. That's her problem." He stopped at the window and stared at the cars going by on the highway.

He still wondered who the man was she had been having

drinks with when he saw her at the tapas place. Had she already moved on, and that's why she hadn't wanted to fix their relationship?

He didn't believe that for one second, but knowing the truth didn't stop the acidic burn of jealousy from eating him up from the inside out. Maybe he shouldn't have come at her with so much anger, but he had been pissed off because she had been ignoring his texts.

Because of traffic, he had shown up late to her job. When he saw her car parked in the lot, he realized she had to be somewhere in the vicinity—or he hoped so. Then he found her calmly sipping a chocolate martini with another man while he was going crazy missing her, and something inside him snapped.

He deeply regretted his behavior, especially since photos of them arguing on the sidewalk had shown up online. The articles identified Audra as the woman he'd gone to dinner with months ago and speculated about a love triangle between him, her, and Nami.

"You do understand why she might be keeping her distance, don't you?" Chadwick asked.

"Whose side are you on?" Damon demanded.

"I'm on your side, son, but I also know you can be less than forthcoming with information."

Damon sank onto the sofa and let his head fall back. "I know my limitations when it comes to communicating, and I'm working on getting better. But as soon as she sent me the text, I reached out to explain. I didn't avoid her."

"True, but you were quite the ladies' man before you became involved with this young lady, so surely you can understand her doubts."

"That's in the past. I'm not that man anymore."

"It seems she's not so sure."

Damon blew out a frustrated breath. "Doesn't matter now. We're done," he muttered.

How could everything have gotten so messed up? One minute he was in a dream relationship with his woman in the stands during his home games, and the next he was dismissed and cut off.

"For the record, she had no reason to doubt me. We talked all the time, and for months I hadn't been seen with anyone else but her."

"I suppose her relationship with her daughter's father didn't help."

Damon had told Chadwick about Audra's problems with her ex.

"He's the one who sent her the link," Damon informed him.

"He was trying to create problems."

"Worked like a charm."

Damon's gaze landed on the set of colorful pillows Audra had suggested he buy after their first date. He'd also purchased a few other items she suggested, including plants that didn't need constant attention since he traveled so much.

"You need the greenery," she had said. "They add visual interest, and bonus, studies show having plants reduces your stress levels."

The silence on the other end of the phone forced him to reflect on his true feelings, and the anger and frustration drained out of him.

"I lost her."

His father didn't respond right away.

"Sounds like you're in love," he finally said.

There it was—the truth Damon had been avoiding all along. What he felt for Audra was undeniable and unlike anything he'd ever experienced with another woman. It wasn't just attraction or fleeting passion—it was deeper and terrified him as much as it pulled him in.

There was so much more he could have said—so much more he *should* have said. He should have told Audra that he loved her. He should have said the thought of living without her was unbearable.

He would never wake up next to her warm body again or reach out in the middle of the night to pull her closer and press his nose into the curve of her neck. He couldn't believe he'd never see the laughter in her eyes or listen to one of her funny stories about her daughter or something a member of her family had done.

He wanted her at the condo when he came home. He wanted surprise dinners that she had cooked, and he wanted to shower her with everything her heart desired. There was so much more he wanted to do for and with her, but they were done.

"You're sure there's nothing you can do? You were happy with her. I could tell this relationship was different," Chadwick said.

"She's stubborn as hell. The truth is, she didn't want to get involved with me in the first place. I spent weeks trying to get her attention. She was worried I'd be like her daughter's father. The guy's a real piece of work. He had a good woman like Audra that he let go because he's busy living the rock star life. Meanwhile, his adorable daughter never sees him because he apparently can't find time to spend with her." Men like Kerry disgusted him.

"So it's truly over?" his father asked.

"Yes. It's over."

A few more minutes passed in conversation before Damon ended the call and sauntered into the bedroom. He walked over to the dresser and opened the drawer filled with Audra's blouses, slacks, and other clothing. This was everything she'd left behind, minus a few accessories like purses and a couple of pairs of shoes he had placed in a box in the closet.

With a clenched jaw, he retrieved the box and piled her clothes on top of her other belongings. Each item was a piece of her, a reminder of the days and nights she spent at his place, turning his bare, empty condo into a warm space filled with joy.

There was nothing else of hers in the room, so he emptied the bathroom drawer that held her toiletries and removed her vitamins from the medicine cabinet. He tossed all of those in the box, as well.

He exhaled slowly, his chest tightening as his gaze lingered on the contents.

Baseball season was almost over, and the Braves would play their last game in a couple of weeks. After the season ended, he'd contact Claudia to send a message to Audra. Tell her to come pick up her things, or he could send them to her—whatever she preferred.

Once her personal belongings were out of his home, that would be the end. Maybe that was why he hadn't returned her things yet.

He released a bitter laugh.

Her clothes leaving his home signaled the end of them for good. After that, there would be no reason for them to have contact with each other. Her absence would become permanent, not only in his house, but in his life—leaving a void he feared he'd never be able to fill.

Chapter Twenty-Two

What am I doing here?

Audra stood beside her car, her gaze lifting to encompass Damon's condominium complex. She could hardly breathe, her heart was racing so fast. She hadn't seen him in six weeks—in the flesh, anyway.

She had watched a couple of his games, rooting for him and the team, but seeing him had been unbearably painful—the heaviness of longing stifling her under its weight.

When Claudia said he'd sent a message about picking up her belongings or having them mailed to her, she jumped at the chance to come pick them up.

Pathetic.

She could have even asked him to leave the box with the concierge, but she wanted to see him. Who could blame her? She hadn't stopped loving him. She hadn't stopped thinking about him or missing him. Every day without Damon was like standing under storm clouds, yearning for the sun to break through and chase away the chill in her bones.

She entered the building and greeted the doorman.

"Hello, Ms. Connor," he replied with a nod.

She took the elevator to Damon's floor and then stood outside his door, staring at the gold numbers—eleven-fifty. This was where it had all started, and this was where it would end.

She rang the doorbell and waited.

The door opened, and Damon stood before her in a cream shirt that molded to his defined chest and showed off his biceps and tattooed arms.

"Hey," she said.

"Hey."

"I'm here for the box." Stomach tight, Audra half-expected him to shove the box of clothes into her chest and send her away.

Instead, he stepped aside and widened the door, silently inviting her in. She crossed the threshold and spotted the cardboard box on the floor near one of the sofas.

"You want to check and make sure everything is in there? I can help you take it down when you're done," he said.

"Sure, thanks." The box was large and probably heavy, so she wouldn't mind the help.

Audra crouched in front of it and did a cursory inspection of the contents, unconcerned if everything was in there. Nothing she had left at his place was irreplaceable.

Standing, she rested her hands on her hips. "That looks like everything."

"Good." His gaze flicked over her.

She had taken extra care with her appearance. Fall had ushered in cooler weather, so she wore a cropped jacket over a plum-colored blouse and tight jeans that showed off her ass. She had also made sure her hair looked fabulous—fixing it into voluminous curls that cascaded around her face and onto her shoulders.

"You been okay?" he asked.

She nodded, his considerable attention leaving her tongue-tied.

A wary pause bloomed between them.

Damon cleared his throat. "How's Little Bit doing?"

Audra smiled at the nickname he had given Kerilyn. "She's fine, keeping me on my toes, as usual. She's doing well in school."

"That's nothing new," Damon said.

"No, it's not," Audra admitted proudly. "She asks about you."

A pained expression crossed his face. "What do you tell her?"

"That you have to travel a lot, and..." Her breath hitched as her chest burned with emotion. "The last time I told her that, she looked sad, and I know she was feeling the same disappointment she experiences when her dad doesn't have time for her—and it's my fault. Maybe I shouldn't have introduced you. Maybe I shouldn't have ended things between us. I... I thought a clean break was best, but now I'm..." Her voice broke, and a runaway tear streamed down her cheek.

Damon quickly closed the small space between them and clasped her face in his big hands. "Do you want to take the box, leave, and we never see each other again? Or do you want to try again? Because that's what I want. I want you."

Audra took a quivering breath. "I want you too," she said in a trembling whisper. "Everything I did—the lack of trust, cutting you off, was because I didn't want to be what I had been with my ex. *Weak.* Giving in. I made a fool of myself over him. The harder I tried, the less he wanted me, and looking back, I behaved like such an idiot. He didn't want the life I wanted—or at least, he didn't want it with me. So I needed to be tough this time—to protect my sanity. That's why I had to cut you off, Damon, because I was worried I'd give in and make a fool of myself again." Her lower lip trembled. "I'm sorry."

She saw nothing but empathy in his face. "I'm sorry too. I should have told you about the damn party with Nami right away."

"It doesn't matter anymore. I don't care. I miss you."

They moved at the same time, and their mouths connected in a searing, sensual kiss. Audra sighed happily as their tongues touched, reigniting the flame that had extinguished inside her.

Straining onto her toes, she let her fingers climb into his hair so she could caress the curly strands and smooth her hand down the back of his strong neck. She had missed touching him, loving on him, feeling every inch of his tall frame pressed against her.

They stumbled toward the bedroom, hastily stripping away their clothes and shoes along the way. Standing beside the bed, Audra flattened against Damon and lost herself in the erotic sensation of skin on skin.

"I love you," Damon said in a taut whisper against her neck, his hands moving lower to cup her bottom.

Audra jerked back and stared at him. "Wh-what did you say?"

His slumberous eyes gazed down at her. Whenever he looked at her like that, it made the blood in her veins pump hotter. "I'm in love with you, Audra."

She swallowed the lump in her throat. "I love you so much," she admitted in a whisper.

A faint smile tucked into the corners of his lips. Then he kissed her hard, and they fell onto the bed as they devoured each other with feverish kisses and roaming hands.

Audra wrapped her legs around his backside and clenched her arms around his neck. His growl of satisfaction filled her ears as he sank his teeth into her soft earlobe and sucked.

She was overheating, dying from the exquisite pleasure of his amorous kisses and touches. She had missed the sensation of his weight on her and his warm breath on her skin. Reaching between them, she took him in her hand and stroked his rigid flesh. Damon shivered above her and buried his face in her neck, his butt tightening beneath the heel of her foot.

"Now. I need you now, baby." His voice was a guttural plea.

Audra moaned, grinding against him in blatant invitation. Shoving his fingers into her silky hair, Damon surged into her with a low growl, and she gasped as electrifying shocks raced through her. He set the pace with rhythmic thrusts of his hips, rocking her on the mattress, forcing her throat muscles to expel whimpering cries.

Gasping and panting, Audra tightened her legs around Damon while her hands swept over his broad back and shoulders. Throwing back her head, she surrendered to the pleasure of his powerful body claiming hers. When his pace increased, she kept time with him, biting her lip as she savored each deep, deliberate stroke.

"You got that good shit, baby. *That good shit*," Damon groaned.

Angling his hips, he hit her spot, and Audra screamed and clawed his muscular back. She knew for sure they must have heard her all the way down in the parking lot.

"That's it. Come for me, baby," Damon coaxed huskily.

That was all it took. Her intimate muscles contracted around him, and he swelled inside her. Her thighs trembled around his hips, and they came at the same time, bodies bucking against each other, their cries filling the air in the room.

Damon collapsed on top of Audra, and she welcomed his weight. It had been so long since she experienced the pressure of his solid body between her thighs that she didn't want to let him go.

Winded and shaken, she closed her eyes and let her thundering heart slowly return to a normal pace. She pressed her cheek against Damon's and savored the scruff of his beard against her soft skin.

He kissed the underside of her jaw and then her chest before easing from between her legs.

"Well," he said. "Welcome back."

"That was quite the welcome."

"I do what I can." As if he couldn't help himself, he dropped another kiss on her lips.

Enjoying the contact, Audra held his face between her hands to prolong it. Briefly, she swept the tip of her tongue along his lower lip, and he moaned.

"I missed you," she whispered.

"Missed you, too, baby." Damon rolled off the bed and strolled toward the bathroom.

Audra admired his graceful walk and the beauty of his muscular body and thought about how lucky she was. He returned from the bathroom with a warm washcloth. After they cleaned up, they lay facing each other under the covers.

"You know I'm never letting you go again, right?" Damon asked, rubbing his knuckles along the slope of her cheek.

"I don't know, the makeup sex might be worth it," Audra teased.

"Nah, we need to find another way to have crazy good sex," he said.

She let out a little laugh and smoothed her palm over his chest. She never grew tired of touching him.

Damon frowned as he looked at her. "Everything okay?"

Despite their time apart, he was still attuned to her moods.

Audra licked her lips. "I have something to tell you."

He sobered. "You're making me nervous. What's wrong?"

Her mother's words came back to her: *When the right man comes along, he'll show you through his actions, not just his words—how important you are to him.* She was about to find out how important she was to Damon.

"I don't know how to say this because I can't believe it happened again."

He raised up on his elbow. "What's happened again?"

Audra took a deep breath and closed her eyes. When she opened them, she looked directly into Damon's face.

"I'm pregnant."

Chapter Twenty-Three

Audra looked at him with fear in her eyes. "Did you hear me? Say something."

Damon sat up in the bed. "Yes, I heard you."

"We weren't always careful, like just now," she explained, as if he didn't know how babies were made.

"When did you find out?"

She sat up, holding the sheet to her breasts. "Coincidentally, the same day you contacted Claudia and sent the message. I was at the doctor's office when she called me."

"Did you plan to tell me?"

"Yes, of course."

He nodded, satisfied with the answer, and slipped from the bed. "We need to get dressed. I can't have this conversation naked."

They moved quietly through the condo, collecting their discarded clothes and putting them back on. During those few minutes, Damon's mind raced with possibilities.

A father. He couldn't believe it.

Finally, they sat down on the sofa facing the balcony, and he took Audra's hand. She looked nervous.

"Why do you look like you're about to throw up?" he asked.

"Because I'm pregnant again. My parents are going to kill me."

"Then let's get married."

Her eyes went wide. "What? No."

"Why not? We love each other."

"Damon, I appreciate the offer, but this is sudden. We weren't planning to get married five minutes ago."

"Plans change. You adjust."

"We're talking about a *baby* and *marriage*. Those are major decisions and life-changing events. We can't make these decisions lightly."

"I'm not making this decision lightly." A smile broke out on his face. "We're having a baby. That's good news."

Clearly, she hadn't expected him to say that. She shot him a look of confusion. "How is this good news?"

"Because we're in love, and we're about to have a baby."

His gaze dropped to her midsection, and his smile widened. He hadn't noticed any difference when they made love, but eventually, her waistline would expand with his child.

Audra eased her hand from his. "Damon, you do know what me being pregnant means, right? That means you're going to be a father. That means all kinds of other responsibilities besides playing ball. When you have a kid, your whole life changes. Forget about sleeping in on your days off. A baby doesn't care if it's one a.m. or one p.m. When they're ready to eat or have their diaper changed, they will scream the whole house down until their needs are satisfied. Don't get me started on teething.

"A baby causes strain on the best of relationships, and we haven't been together that long. Less than six months. We're still getting to know each other. I haven't met your parents or anyone else in your family yet! Weekend trips like the one we took to the retreat are out the window. We were only able to do that because my daughter is older. I won't leave our child with other people to take care of for a weekend when they're that little.

"And they're expensive!" Audra continued. "They need clothes they'll outgrow within months, there's private school if we want to go that route, college down the road—and everything in between. Being a parent changes you forever, and it's not an easy job. Your life is no longer your own because your child takes over your life. Do you understand that?"

She had said a mouthful, but nothing she said had changed his mind.

"I understand more than you know, and despite everything you've said, I'm still excited. I'm willing to put in the work because the reward is great." He leaned toward her. "I want someone to look at me like the world revolves around me. I want to take care of our son or daughter and protect them and let them know how much they're loved."

He paused as emotion swelled inside him.

"I'm looking forward to their first smile, their first steps, and when I get to teach them to ride a bike. I'll teach them to throw a ball and work with their hands. We'll go biking, swimming, camping—everything. I'm looking forward to a little you or a little me—a combination of both of us. I already know it's not always going to be easy, Audra, but I want this baby, and I want this baby with you."

She looked stunned, her mouth hanging halfway open.

Damon continued. "You've already shown me what kind of mother you'll be. I can't think of anyone else I'd want to have a child with, and one thing's for sure: my kid will *never, ever* doubt that they're loved."

Her brow puckered, and she placed a hand on his jaw. "What happened to you when you were younger, Damon?" she asked softly.

His jaw tightened as he struggled with a surge of emotion. Then he pulled back. "You don't want to hear my dirt."

"If we're going to raise a child together, I think I deserve to know your background." Her voice was gentle, cautious.

Damon stood abruptly and went to stand in front of one of the windows. He heard her get up, and she came to stand beside him.

He didn't want to talk about his childhood and had effectively kept her in the dark this entire time. Turning away, he returned to the sofa and sat down, unsure where to begin—unsure if he wanted to begin.

Audra followed him again, but this time she straddled his thighs.

"Audra…" he said in a warning tone.

"Talk to me. Please." She cupped either side of his face in her hands and forced eye contact. Sympathy filled her eyes.

Damon knew he had to open up, but damn, was it hard. Finally, he pushed the words past his lips. "I'm adopted."

"I don't remember that in any of the articles I read about you."

He dipped his gaze. "I don't talk about it. Dena and Chadwick Foster are my parents, and that's all that matters. The same way all your siblings are your siblings, whether they're related to you or not." She had told him that the first night they went out to Prime Table.

Audra nodded her understanding. "Do you mind sharing how you ended up getting adopted?"

His body tensed. He didn't want to tell her but sensed this time he wouldn't be let off the hook.

"I grew up in an abusive home. My father terrorized us

with punches... and kicks... yelling and weapons—knives, a gun, a baseball bat. Didn't matter to him, and he smashed stuff all the time. He was the one who destroyed my Spiderman kite, for no reason except he was in a bad mood, and I came home from the park at the wrong time. I don't remember a time when I wasn't scared to go home from school or anywhere, for that matter. I was always worried that I'd say the wrong thing and set him off. He used to beat my mother too. Eventually, I was removed from the apartment, and that's when I met the woman who would become my mom. She was my social worker. My biological parents gave up their parental rights, confirming that they had never wanted me." He swallowed as the memory of their rejection tightened his chest. "But Dena, my mother, she wanted me. Which is crazy, because looking back, I can admit I was a handful. I don't know what made my case special compared to all the others she had handled. Luckily, my father was open to adopting a troubled eleven-year-old."

Damon stared unseeing at a point beyond Audra.

"Damon, I... I'm so sorry that happened to you. I had no idea."

He lifted his gaze to hers. "I don't want your pity, Audra. I'm fine now."

"I don't think you are," she said gently. "Have you thought about going to therapy?"

He let out a scoffing laugh. "For what? That shit don't work. I don't need a therapist. I know who I am, and I know what kind of father I'll be."

"I wasn't suggesting you wouldn't be a good father," Audra said hastily. "But it's obvious that what happened to you still affects—"

"I'm fine," Damon insisted in a harder voice. "I'm going to be an involved father. Not only to the baby you're carrying, but to Kerilyn too. When we get married, I won't treat her any differently than the kids we have together. We already know we're in sync in a lot of ways. I'm not worried or scared. I want this."

She stared at him for a moment, as if she couldn't believe her ears. Then, slowly, relief crossed her face. "This is the real reason why they call you The Flash. You move fast. You don't waste any time."

"Why waste time when you know what you want? I love you. You love me. I know it's scary because we didn't have plans to get married and raise a family right now."

"It's very scary," Audra admitted.

"But it feels right—don't it?"

The happy smile that broke out on her face was the only answer he needed. "Yes, it does. You know, my mother told me once that there's no timeframe for love. For some people, it happens quickly. For others, it takes longer. The only common feature is that love grows. You might not be aware of it, and then one day... one day you need that other person in your life, because your life won't be complete without them."

"That's exactly how I feel about you. I want this, Audra. You and our baby. It's not too soon. It's right on time."

He pulled her in for a deep, heartfelt kiss.

Despite the fame, wealth, and the opportunity to do what he loved, he had never felt completely satisfied. That changed with Audra, and he was young—younger than he had expected to be when he got married and started a family—but all he saw was a future with her. Nothing else mattered because his life was finally going to be complete. He'd have a family of his own.

They spent the rest of the night discussing their dreams and marital expectations. Their belief systems and desires for the future were very compatible.

Damon had no doubt that getting married and starting a life together would be the right decision.

Epilogue

Audra woke up, shifted, and checked the bassinet beside the bed. It was empty, and for a split second, she panicked before she saw movement out the corner of her eye.

She could just make out her husband's shadowy form in the dark, seated in a chair in the corner and holding their son.

She moved again, wincing and making a sound in her throat when pain shot through her.

"You okay, baby? You need anything?" Damon asked.

She had given birth two days ago, and he was consistently attentive. "No, I'm fine. You're holding Junior again?"

"He made a noise, so I checked on him. I didn't want him to start crying and wake you up. He stopped whining when I picked him up."

"He's going to be so spoiled."

"Nothing wrong with that," Damon said. "Now I understand why you used to stare at Kerilyn. I can't stop staring at this kid."

With her eyes adjusted to the dark, Audra could see Damon better as he gazed down at the bundle in his arms.

"I'm never gonna hurt you," he promised in a whisper.

Her heart seized with pain. Damon's abusive upbringing often crossed her mind. She had grown up in a loving household, and her heart broke thinking about the trauma he had endured.

"What time are your parents coming in the morning?"

Dena and Chadwick were coming to see their grandson in person, though they had already been bombarded with plenty of photos and videos—courtesy of their doting son.

"Their flight lands at ten. I'm going to meet them at the airport."

His parents were going to stay at a hotel nearby. With Audra, the baby, and Kerilyn in the condo, they didn't have space for his parents, which prompted Damon to start looking for a bigger place. They discussed buying a property with a big yard for their future five kids to run around in.

He continued to hold their son for a little longer and then finally placed him in the bassinet on Audra's side of the bed. A handmade teddy bear with a bejeweled bow sat on the table, one of several gifts from Monica, who was over the moon at becoming an aunt again. Her sister had playfully told her to keep the teddy bear nearby to watch over their son, and Audra adhered to her request.

Damon climbed in bed beside her. "Are you good?"

"Always, when I'm next to you."

She closed her eyes, content in the knowledge that she was loved. Her parents didn't kill her when she announced her second pregnancy, and Kerilyn had been excited about becoming a big sister. The first time she saw her little brother, she cried happy tears. The transition from the mansion to

Damon's condo had been a drastic change, but she was now fully adjusted with her stepfather loving her the way she'd always craved.

Audra had gotten everything she wanted, and she looked forward to a happy, magical future with the man she loved.

An Excerpt from Audra (Family Ties, book 3)

"What did you think of my speech?" Damon asked.

He and Audra entered the house from the garage and stepped into the kitchen. Tonight, he accepted an award as the year's Sports Humanitarian for his charitable donations and the time he spent mentoring and coaching young boys.

"Like I told you weeks ago, it was good," she said, making her way to the foyer.

He followed her up the stairs. The house was quiet because their three children weren't there. They hadn't been sure what time they would get home, so the kids spent the night at her mother's before they went to the event.

"Good as in okay, or good as in I killed it?" Damon asked.

He always practiced his speeches in front of Audra, and she gave him pointers, not only for the delivery but for the speech itself. He trusted her writing skills, and when she gave a suggestion, he made the revisions. But practice in the den was a whole different animal than delivering in front of a room filled with people hanging on his every word.

"You killed it," Audra said.

They entered the master bedroom at the end of the hall.

"You're right, I killed it."

Audra flipped on the light and illuminated their bedroom.

She slanted a glance over her shoulder. Her hair swished with the movement, bone straight and shimmering black from a silk press. "Careful, your head is growing," she teased.

He laughed, watching as she stepped out of her heels with fluid movements. Feminine and casually graceful. His wife was so sexy.

"You said I did good," he reminded her.

"Mhmm. Actually, you did fantastic, hon. I have to give you some sugar for that."

With the shoes dangling from her fingers, she stood on tiptoe and kissed his bearded cheek, her lips soft as rose petals. The blood leaped under his skin. They hadn't had sex in a while, but maybe he'd get lucky tonight.

He shrugged off his jacket and tossed it onto one of the chairs in front of the fireplace.

Like the rest of the house, Audra had handled the decor. The master bedroom was designed with an eye for comfort and simple elegance, with a California king bed and a custom-built tufted headboard reaching almost to the high ceiling. With no television in the room, the focal point was the fireplace surrounded by polished alabaster tiles, above which hung an abstract painting from an up-and-coming local artist. Teal armchairs and a cocktail table rested in front of the fireplace. Throw pillows and drapes in cool colors like green and blue contrasted against the white and tan in the bedsheets and on the walls.

"I'm very proud of you." Audra went into her large walk-in closet.

Damon went to stand in the doorway, his mouth watering as she slipped the black dress down her arms and stepped out of it, revealing skin the color of deepest, darkest brown sugar and the luscious curves of her hourglass figure. She wore a black lace bra and matching thong, which disappeared between her ample butt cheeks.

"As long as you think I did well, that's all that matters," he said. "By the way, I forgot to tell you that Simon texted me during the program. TAG Heuer contacted him. They want to re-up my contract."

Ever since he quit playing baseball, Damon expanded his income through modeling, licensing deals, and investments. The flexibility of being able to set his own schedule and not having to answer to anyone gave him more time to spend with his family. His friend and attorney, Simon Finch, negotiated the modeling and licensing deals.

"Are you interested?" Audra hung up her dress and started removing her bra and jewelry.

His body stirred with desire as he watched her disrobe, an erection straining the front of his pants. "Definitely. I like the watches, so they're an easy sell."

He promoted the TAG Heuer sports collection, and a drawer in his closet was filled with their watches. At the moment, he wore the Carrera Porsche Chronograph Special Edition timepiece—the most expensive one in the line.

"I'm guessing you told Simon yes?" Audra slipped on a cute white pajama set, made up of shorts and a top with thin straps.

"I did," Damon answered.

She came toward him, a smile reflected in her pretty dark eyes, her round face accentuated by sinfully full lips.

When she exited the closet, he gently tugged her close. Slipping an arm around her waist, he kissed her on the mouth.

He had only meant to be affectionate, but she smelled good, wearing a rose and orange blossom perfume. The combination of that scent and her soft body inflamed his desire. But as he deepened the kiss, she tensed in his arms and pulled back, placing a hand on his chest.

"Honey, I need to wash off my makeup."

"Wash it off later. I'm trying to get a little something, something," he said with a wicked grin. One hand coasted low and grabbed her ass.

Audra became more tense and edged away from his hand, her face apologetic. "Not tonight. It's been a long day, and I'm tired. I'm not in the mood."

Heat flamed Damon's neck, and he reluctantly released her. "Seems you're hardly ever in the mood nowadays," he remarked, keeping his voice neutral.

He didn't want to start a fight, but she pulled away from him more often than not lately.

"That's not true. We had sex a couple weeks ago," Audra said.

"A month ago," Damon corrected.

Her eyebrows drew together. "Has it been that long?"

"Yeah."

She dodged his eyes and veered toward the bathroom. "Oh," she said in a low voice.

Damon didn't respond, instead going to his own walk-in closet and removing his clothes with frustrated yanks. He changed into pajama bottoms, then returned to the bedroom where he removed the throw pillows from the bed and placed them on a shelf of the armoire, below the extra pillows, blankets, and sheets. He paused, eyes resting on the locked box on the bottom shelf that contained "toys" for when they were feeling a little kinky. It contained a couple of vibrators, Ben Wa balls, a vinyl whip, nipple clamps, lubricant, fur-lined hand-cuffs, and a mask. He couldn't remember the last time they had unlocked the box and used any of the contents.

After he turned off the light, he slipped under the thin blanket and lay supine on the mattress with his arms folded behind his head and his penis at half-mast.

Audra used to enjoy his touch. Hell, she used to initiate sex. He never dreamed he'd see the day when she talked about sex as if once every two weeks was sufficient. Desire burned through him at the slightest brush of her body against his, but if he was being brutally honest, she behaved as if she no longer wanted him to touch her at all, and his ego was taking a beating.

She exited the bathroom, and in the ambient light, he saw her rubbing lotion on her hands and elbows. His eyes followed her until she slipped under the covers with him.

"Maybe we can do something tomorrow night," she said.

The words chafed.

Pity sex.

"Nah, I'm good. If you don't want to, you don't have to," Damon said, staring up into the darkness.

"It's not that I don't want to," Audra said in a small voice.

Coulda fooled me, he thought.

"Are you upset?" she asked.

"No."

"Talk to me."

"About what?"

"Tell me what you're thinking."

He smothered a sigh. She always complained that he didn't talk enough. He knew that but couldn't bring himself to open up more.

"You don't want to know what I'm thinking, Audra."

"I do."

"No, you don't." He rolled onto his side, away from her. "Good night."

"Damon—"

"Good night, Audra."

Quiet filled the room for a while.

"Good night," she finally whispered.

Also by Delaney Diamond

More from the Family Ties series!

Audra - The Prequel (Family Ties #0)

Thanks to an unexpected pregnancy, they both realize that some risks are worth taking—especially when love is at stake.

Ethan (Family Ties #1)

After seven years together, one night, Skye broaches the subject of marriage and learns the devastating truth. Ethan has no intention of marrying her.

Monica (Family Ties #2)

Andre is engaged to marry the daughter of the man who gave him a chance when no one else would, but seeing Monica causes old feelings to resurface and calls his plans into question.

Audra (Family Ties #3)

When Audra asks for a divorce, she and Damon are forced to face the truth about their marriage. Can they rekindle the fire in the relationship... before it's too late?

Bruno (Family Ties #4)

When Bruno hires a matchmaking service to find him a wife, sparks fly between him and the matchmaker, blurring the lines between love and professionalism.

***

More family series are available!

Visit my Books page to learn about all my books and the

Johnson Family

Brooks Family

Hawthorne Family

* * *

Audiobook samples and free short stories available at www.delaneydi-amond.com.

About the Author

Delaney Diamond is the USA Today Bestselling Author of sensual, passionate romance novels. Originally from the U.S. Virgin Islands, she now lives in Atlanta, Georgia. She reads romance novels, mysteries, thrillers, and a fair amount of nonfiction. When she's not busy reading or writing, she's in the kitchen trying out new recipes, dining at one of her favorite restaurants, or traveling to an interesting locale.

Enjoy free reads on her website. Join her mailing list to get sneak peeks, notices of sale prices, and find out about new releases.

Join her mailing list
www.delaneydiamond.com

facebook.com/DelaneyDiamond
instagram.com/delaneydiamondbooks
x.com/DelaneyDiamond
pinterest.com/delaneydiamond

www.ingramcontent.com/pod-product-compliance
Lightning Source LLC
Chambersburg PA
CBHW051242170626
46809CB00004B/1448